I0569758

Taming the Beast

MASTERING
THE BEAST

TINA DONAHUE

Mastering the Beast
ISBN # 978-1-83943-814-1
©Copyright Tina Donahue 2018
Cover Art by Posh Gosh ©Copyright June 2018
Interior text design by Claire Siemaszkiewicz
Totally Bound Publishing

Published in 2019 by Totally Bound Publishing, United Kingdom.

MASTERING
THE BEAST

Dedication

To lovers of ménage
who like their romances hot and spicy.

Chapter One

Zoe stormed toward a treatment room, ready to rumble.

As the top enforcer at From Crud to Stud, *the* New Orleans' makeover service for supernatural beings, she didn't take lip or attitude from anyone. She'd made that fatal mistake in the past. First with hard-nosed villagers during the Salem witch trials, which had been way worse than the fluff shown on the History Channel. Then with Satan after he'd wooed her to Hell using his typical bait-and-switch scheme. What a creep he'd turned out to be.

Twice in her existence, she'd let guys determine her future. No more. She was her own woman now, uninterested in men. Her work here was all she needed, guided by her determination to do things the mortal way—suffer and endure, no supernatural powers allowed.

She pushed open the door and faced a sickly looking vamp who sported a pasty complexion and a man bun. Hardly a babe magnet. Only fierce dedication and hard work would turn him into Mr. Charm. "Yo. On the table. Now." Before the staffers helped him to suppress his inner beast, she had to strap him down. An easy-peasy job for a reformed demon with hardcore ways.

He licked his fangs flirtatiously. Some might say hungrily. "Hey. I'm—"

"I'm not going to ask again."

"Easy, cupcake. I'm just trying to make conversation. What's your name?"

"Kim Kardashian."

"Yeah?" He regarded her scrawny figure. "You changed. Like a lot."

"It's an illusion. Call it my work uniform. Once I'm on my own time, I blossom."

"Cool."

They circled each other, both ready to pounce.

Given his powers, he struck first and sank his teeth into her neck.

She tapped her foot but let him do his thing.

"Gah." He gagged and recoiled. "Damn, you taste like hell."

Surprise, surprise. "Time for you to learn some manners. Good thing you came to us."

He eyed a female staffer strolling by and gave her a toothy grin.

Zoe got in his face. "Park your butt over there now."

"When I'm good and ready, sweetheart." He craned his neck to watch the staffer. "Run along."

Zoe rammed her saddle shoe into his foot and her elbow into his gut, wrestled him to the table then strapped him in so he'd never get free. Not even if he morphed into a freaking bat. His frustrated hiss mingled with a reaper's wail, zombie grunts and were howls.

Lovely sounds, ordinarily. However, tonight something was off, the evening heavy with tension that breathed danger. Similar to when another demon slunk nearby.

Warily, she approached the last two treatment rooms. Both were empty. The walls bore claw marks from former inhabitants.

Maybe she was overreacting due to the calendar date. Halloween approached, the dumbest and most inaccurate holiday ever.

Heather, a healer and the good fairy receptionist there, had decorated her desk with plastic skulls. Fake cobwebs hung from the faux gas fixtures. Rubber spiders stuck to the coral walls and spelled out *Boo!* on the artificial brick floor.

Zoe resisted the urge to roll her eyes or say anything unkind, since Heather was her BFF.

Heather smiled adoringly at Daemon, a former satyr. He'd come to the service more than a year ago to ditch his horns, tail and hooves in order to look fully human so he could boogie with mortal babes. Not only did he work there now as an enforcer, he and Heather had shacked up, their love more enduring than Romeo and Juliet's. They laughed easily and gazed at each other with tenderness and respect whenever they weren't busy making out like sex-starved teens.

Loneliness tightened Zoe's chest. She ached from unexpected longing but shook it off.

Romance wasn't what she needed or could risk. She'd learned that brutal truth centuries ago when she'd had wanted one guy, just one, more than life itself. What a hot mess *that* had turned out to be, especially after she'd sold her soul to get his affection. Talk about false advertising. What she'd ended up with was a one-way ticket to Hell along with Satan's negligent shrug and pissy explanation about what had happened.

"It all boils down to free will." He'd grinned. "The guy doesn't want you. What can I do?"

Satan made first-class louses look like Prince Charming.

However, he had taught her an important lesson. No way would she ever fall for another man and give him her heart, if she'd had one. These past years, she'd sworn off dating, companionship and especially sex even though celibacy was killing her. Especially tonight.

The only thing she couldn't figure out was why.

"Zoe." Becca, another BFF and the half-mortal witch who owned this place, motioned her to the other hall. "Can we have a word in my office?"

That same edgy feeling returned and grew stronger. She expected a demon to pounce from behind the feathery ferns or potted plants that adorned the reception area.

No one was there.

"Now?" Becca led the way. Her harem pants rode low on her voluptuous hips and swished around her legs. Her tie-front crop top hugged her ample boobs. Both garments were iridescent blue that matched her eyes.

In her office, she gestured Zoe to the needlepoint sofa that faced the antique desk. Displayed on the cabinet behind it were numerous photos of Becca and Eric, a minor god she'd met and had fallen in love with when he'd come there for treatment.

Melancholy hit, followed by dread. Zoe worried another staffer had found her man and now that guy was going to work here like Daemon. A new enforcer would cut even deeper into her territory. The only thing she had left.

Rather than sitting, she squared her shoulders prepared to defend her turf.

Becca smiled cautiously. A sure sign she wasn't certain what to do, like when she practiced her witchcraft. Poor thing had been studying hard but managed more misses than hits when she concocted spells or potions. If not for her mom, Rowena, helping with those things, she would have been shit outta luck.

Zoe lifted her chin and got bolder than she felt. "Is this about Constance?"

Another BFF and the resident voodoo priestess here. Given that Constance liked men big time, it was a miracle she hadn't been the first on their team to hook up.

Becca frowned slightly. "What about her?"

"Shouldn't she be in here, too?" Seemed reasonable if she had a once-in-a-lifetime romance to gush about.

"No. She's with a client, removing some of his memories."

Zoe suspected those involved the dude's former girlfriend that Constance wanted him to forget. "So the client is the one she's in love with?"

"Love?" Becca pressed her hand to her chest. "Oh, my God, is she serious about someone? I didn't know she was even dating on a regular basis. What have you heard?"

Confused, Zoe shook her head. "Nothing. Is this about MJ?"

She was a genie who'd used to live in Daemon's ring before he set her free. Currently, she was his and Heather's houseguest and also worked there granting wishes to clients for a price. Like Constance, MJ enjoyed doing the nasty with guys. Little wonder she'd found her man. "She's hooked up with someone?"

"You mean permanently?" Becca's eyes widened. The heavy black makeup surrounding them made them appear larger against her fair skin. "I don't think so. Daemon had to separate her and a were earlier. They were really going at it. Once she left him, she had her eye on a warlock. Have you heard or seen something different?"

"Uh-uh. I thought you knew something and wanted to tell me about it in here."

"Oh…no." She made a face and shook it off. "This is about business. We've been really swamped this year, so I've decided to expand. I've already talked to the building's owner about taking over the entire floor and renovating it for our use."

Zoe's tension drained away. "Cool. You want me to keep the workers in line in between my other stuff?" She slammed her fist against her palm. "I'll be happy to."

Becca stopped fingering her short red hair. "I don't want you to kill yourself by working so hard."

"How could I do that?" She frowned. "I'm already dead, not to mention immortal."

"That's not what I meant." Becca waved her hand dismissively. "I want you to enjoy your work."

That funny feeling returned and made Zoe queasy. "Who says I don't like what I do here? Oh, hey, is this about Daemon horning in on more of my stuff? Uh-uh. He's already keeping the clients in line for the other staff. I don't need him to do that for me. I'm capable. Hell, I'm a better enforcer than him. I do not want him anywhere near my customers."

"No problem. He won't be." Becca cleared her throat. "Stefin, Anatol and Taro will be here for that from now on."

Footfalls rang in the hall.

Three guys strode into Becca's office, their movements fluid and assured. Each looked thirty or so, in mortal years, and had dressed in black, their shirts silk, their boots and pants elegant, like bouncers wear at an elite club.

No one was dancing in here, especially Zoe.

A faint sulfur scent emanated from the unholy trio. Flames flared briefly in their eyes.

Demons. The trouble she'd sensed earlier.

She froze, too stunned to move or speak.

The guy in the middle was easily six-three and nicely muscular, his blond hair shoulder-length. His rough good looks, bronze complexion and stubble put the va-va-voom in virile. Sin filled his light gray eyes, his mood dangerous and predatory.

Her belly fluttered.

He winked.

Disquiet and lust rolled through Zoe. Her legs went watery.

The guy on the right proved equally tall and powerfully built. Beautiful, he had rich-chocolate skin, dark eyes and long hair worn in dreadlocks.

Those babies would feel awesome gliding across her naked boobs and thighs — until he screwed her over like every other male had done.

She steeled herself against his allure.

He smiled.

A freaking dimple dented his right cheek, his grin an unusual combination of boyish mischief and raw sensuality.

Her pussy creamed.

Hot didn't begin to describe the last guy's masculine features, deep-blue eyes and thick auburn hair. Those wavy locks trailed past his ears and curled on his neck. His stubble called to everything female within Zoe, as did his height, big body and the assured way he regarded her.

The guys' enticing sulfur odor enhanced their musky scents, making the mixture wanton and unashamed. Their impressive cocks pushed against their flies.

She bet each of their rods jutted from blond, black or auburn curls.

The room spun.

"Guys." Becca lifted her reddish eyebrows. "This is Zoe."

The introduction seemed to come from far away, Becca's voice muted by the ringing in Zoe's ears. She tried to respond but only managed an odd noise, part grunt, mostly a groan.

Becca edged closer. "Zoe, this is Anatol." She gestured to the black hunk with the dimple. "Stefin." The blond god in the middle winked again. "And Taro." The blue-eyed hottie regarded her intensely. "They're our new enforcers."

Each looked in charge already, their stances saying they wouldn't budge one damn inch for anyone, especially a female demon.

Becca offered a nervous smile. "You'll be working with them from now on."

Working with or for, as in taking orders, yearning helplessly then losing out as she had with the last man in her life?

Like hell.

Stefin had never met a female demon quite like Zoe.

Wispy smoke rose from her narrow shoulders and long black hair. The delightful scent heightened her female musk and proved her outrageous lust to him, her willingness to submit. What a flirtatious display for a demon, playful yet also provocative, rather than in-your-face sexy.

His devilish desire kicked up several notches, thickening his cock and plumping his balls.

Slender as a waif, she was no more than five feet, her exceedingly pale complexion decorated with facial piercings. Two silver studs across her nose, four in her plush lower lip, several rings in her dark eyebrows and one in her left nostril. Despite the heavy-metal look, she'd dressed like a convent schoolgirl in a white, long-sleeved blouse, green plaid skirt that fell to mid-calf, anklet socks and saddle oxfords.

Thrown by her get-up, Stefin leaned toward Becca. "Is she of age?"

Becca shot him a look.

He wasn't certain why. "What?"

"She's twenty-five in mortal years."

"How old is she supernaturally?"

"None of your damn business." Zoe's comment was throaty as all get out, a big voice for such a small girl.

She stood toe-to-toe with him. Her forehead barely reached his pecs. "In case you haven't noticed, I'm still in this room. I can hear you, mister."

What a firecracker, calling him mister rather than Master. Not that it mattered. In very little time, he'd woo her and she'd want nothing more than to submit to carnal hunger, her nudity displayed for his delight and their pleasure.

Flames danced in her black eyes, bottomless pools of indecent passion. Smoke spewed from her hair.

Enjoying her arousal, Stefin grinned.

Her frown faded, showing how pretty she was, her features soft and longing as a woman's should be.

He leaned down to her. "Tell me how old you are supernaturally and I'll show you things that will make you smile as you've never done before."

She turned to Becca. "I'm not working with him or them."

Of course not—she was working for them. They'd be patient and loving Masters and she'd be an enthusiastic sub. The way the universe worked. Stefin shrugged. "I agree."

Bewilderment crossed her face, followed by relief then what looked like regret. That emotion he didn't get.

She stepped back.

He followed, or rather pursued, as a man should.

Zoe crossed her arms beneath her small breasts. "You're really asking for it, aren't you?"

She wanted to play. How adorable. The other female demons Stefin had known were bold as hell, getting down and dirty with no flirting or come-ons whatsoever, which made sex perfunctory and too similar to his mortal days. As a product of Russian culture during its bleakest period, he'd experienced sexual equality firsthand, where men were men and women were too, everyone the same. Stoically hard. Endlessly grim. Decidedly sexless. That just wasn't right and couldn't have been what nature had intended. Stefin enjoyed a carnal dance that a man was destined to win simply because he was male.

He offered a mischievous smile. "Asking for what?"

She arched one slender eyebrow. "Don't tempt me."

"I thought I already had."

Was that yearning blurring her gaze?

"Ah, guys." Becca rubbed her neck. "There's work to do. You better get to it. Zoe, please show them the routine."

Smoke belched from her hair.

What other proof did Stefin need of her boundless arousal? She was more than ready for him.

Becca wrung her hands. "Please, Zoe. You know I wouldn't do anything to hurt you, ever. You and I are closer than sisters could ever be. We'd die for each other. Or at least I would since you're already... You know what I mean. I hired extra enforcers as a business decision. It has no reflection on your work. You're the best and always will be. But everyone needs help at times."

A pretty speech. However, it wasn't one Stefin understood. He leaned toward Becca. "The best?" He kept his voice lowered so Zoe couldn't possibly overhear. "Always will be? You couldn't be serious about that now that I'm here. You're trying to appease her, right?"

She glared. "What do you think?"

He hadn't a clue how to answer and sensed it was best to keep his peace for now.

Becca smiled softly at Zoe. "Please show them the ropes?"

She sagged but marched to the door. Her skirt swayed, revealing her calves.

Determined to see far more, Stefin followed and gestured Anatol and Taro to do the same.

In the hall, Anatol elbowed Taro. "I'm surprised Zoe didn't chew off Stefin's balls in there."

"Knowing him, he expects her to lick them."

"After he behaved like a damn Cossack, repeatedly asking her age?" Anatol sniffed. "A woman needs to be wooed before any man can expect obedience. I'll have to show him how it's done."

"You?"

They turned a corner, following Zoe and Stefin past the receptionist who was called Hilary or Hilda or something beginning with an H. Her blouse, skirt and shoes were a uniform white. Coupled with her pale blonde hair and alabaster skin, she was almost too bright to look at.

She smiled sweetly.

Anatol returned her greeting with a pleasant, nonthreatening nod as a gentleman should. Although he'd grown up in Paris slums and had been a notorious thief during his mortal days, he knew how to treat a woman properly and was eager to try his hand with Zoe.

She certainly wasn't what he'd expected.

When Becca had said Zoe was an enforcer here, he'd anticipated a brawny woman whose muscles and facial hair would rival his. Except for her ballsy attitude, she was surprisingly delicate and vulnerable. The moment he and the others had showed up, her lower lip had trembled.

Thankfully, she hadn't wept. If she had…

A woman's tears always made him feel stupid, clumsy and powerless. Hardly the best way to begin his first shift.

Despite Becca's comment about Zoe always being the best, he sensed she worried their presence here had diminished hers.

He wanted to enhance it. There was something about her that reminded him of the woman he'd lost nearly seventy-five years ago when he'd still believed in hope and a future that seemed within reach.

It hadn't worked out then. There'd been too little time and more rotten luck than they'd been able to survive. Now, he had an eternity to pursue whatever and whoever interested or intrigued him. A new lightness brightened his outlook. He kept pace with Zoe.

Her brisk steps caused her hair to bob. She clenched her fists.

Poor girl. Such anguish wasn't necessary.

When he had a chance, he'd uncurl her fingers and press his lips to her palms. He'd slip his tongue inside her mouth to taste the demon she really was and explore her scant curves.

He'd romance then mount her as they both wanted. Once she'd experienced him, she'd surely beg for more.

A reaper rushed into the hall.

Taro reared back.

A staffer raced past, her hair flying. "Hey, you can't leave. Your treatment's not through. Get. Back. Here."

The reaper bounded toward the front door.

Ready to get moving again, Taro elbowed Anatol.

He blinked slowly, his gaze welded to Zoe, his mood distracted and immoral. Like he was fucking her in his mind.

What a hypocrite. From sunrise to sunset, Anatol loved to boast about being the civilized one in their group. To hear him tell it, he knew how to talk, eat, walk and behave in polite company better than anyone alive or dead. When it came to wooing a woman, he had no equal. Not even Casanova or Don Juan could compete. He'd told them that too when they'd run into each other in Hell. He also claimed he'd cut off his own balls before he'd ever be vulgar like Stefin or as uncouth as he considered Taro.

Well, la-di-da. It wasn't Taro's fault he'd lived during this country's frontier period when niceties were in short supply. Breaking the law was practically a religion and the only way to survive if you were dirt poor. Good intentions and sweet talk didn't get you far and sure as blazes didn't fill your belly.

He wasn't proud of what he'd been back then, but he wasn't ashamed, either. Nor did he believe he was clueless when it came to what women wanted. It was remarkably simple and amazingly complicated. They needed tender words, fucking good sex and everlasting commitment.

His belly twisted. He'd never been good at offering his heart. Lovin' and leavin' them had been his style.

Thankfully, women had more options these days than they'd had in the past. They made their own dough, lived their lives and could hook up with men for nothing deeper than a good time, which included BDSM games — dominance, submission, punishment...

Something he'd like to indulge in with Zoe. Damn, she was feisty and would be a delight to tame.

She stopped and faced him and the others.

Taro affected his poker face, unwilling to give away his thoughts.

The flames in Zoe's eyes flashed brightly. She jabbed her thumb at the open door and the room just beyond it. "In there. Don't touch anything. And don't even think about sitting down or getting comfortable in any way, shape or form."

Chapter Two

Zoe tried to calm down, but it was hopeless and ultimately humiliating. While most frustrated demons simply destroyed everything in their path, she restrained herself and played it cool. Or she tried. Every time something pissed her off, smoke poured from her hair and shoulders.

She stifled a cough and refused to bat the sulfurous plumes away, admitting they bugged her. Like what Becca had done. No matter how busy this place was, she shouldn't have hired these great-looking goons.

Zoe didn't need to relax—she craved constant work to keep her mind off sex and how lonely she was despite her desire to feel otherwise. Having these bad boys around tempting her with foolish need wasn't going to make things better.

Annoyed, she followed the guys into her office but kept the door open to prove she didn't trust them. They were too full of themselves, even now. None bothered to glance at her many awards, given for being the best enforcer five years running. In all that time, she'd never pulverized the clients beyond repair, even when they'd deserved it. She'd been strictly professional, giving them nothing more than a few bruises, gashes and broken bones that Heather had healed. For an extra fee.

Those injuries had been good for business. Never had Becca complained about the positive cash flow. Not that such dedication had changed her mind about reducing Zoe's territory here. Nor would the unholy trio be impressed by her successes, or even care.

Stefin sniffed the smoke rising from her shoulders. Excitement darkened his complexion, like she'd emitted the stuff to arouse him.

Anatol took her in from her saddle oxfords to her Peter Pan collar. His breathing picked up, possibly from being turned on.

Taro studied her mouth, his face a mask, telling her nothing.

Wasn't necessary.

They wouldn't find her remotely attractive for the long haul, just as a fast fuck when no one else was available. She was too short, flat, plain and independent. Certainly not the fawning demon they'd probably expected, sporting spike heels, a tight dress and a brain-dead smile while kneeling at their feet, begging them to do her.

They would, too, if she let them.

Zoe fought intolerable longing. Didn't help. Sensuality and raw male power oozed from them and drew her closer. Another step and she'd be near enough to kiss them or do something far less innocent.

The flames in Stefin's eyes burned brightly, or as she liked to call it—hornily. Anatol lost his preoccupied look and met her gaze, his expectant. Taro leaned closer.

So did she, losing her control too easily. Startled, she backed up.

They followed as one, like the damn Rockettes.

Their musk and intense heat enveloped her. In another second, they'd burst into flame from too much carnal hunger. Once they'd satisfied their basest urges, they'd ignore her and pounce on other women. Possibly Heather, maybe even Becca, Constance or MJ, unless MJ attacked them first. That's just the way she was. They were no different, randy with the babes, giving someone as ordinary as Zoe scant attention before they moved on. A repeat of what she'd suffered through with other demons before she turned her existence around for good, making it empty as hell and boring beyond belief. A real downer, but at least she hadn't let her self-respect get crushed again.

"Hold it." Panting, she held up her palm to stop their advance.

They inched closer. Their breaths warmed her fingers.

Unsettled, she dropped her hand and stepped back. "I'm in charge here."

Stefin's patronizing smile nearly wrapped around his ears.

At any other time, that would have made her batshit crazy. Right now, Zoe couldn't manage much anger. She was far too busy fighting pressing need from centuries of not being wanted by men, even those who were lucky to get any female. Stefin was far beyond a hottie, straight into epic. Everything she'd always craved in a guy.

He advanced.

Anatol and Taro followed, both also legendary.

All wanting her as much as she hungered for them. *Wow.* This was unbelievable, which meant too good to be true.

Remembering that, Zoe retreated and bumped into her desk. She considered crawling on it but couldn't. Stefin had already trapped her with his size and determination.

"How you smoke." His thick accent rasped the words, his voice so deep the sounds vibrated in her belly.

Her knees sagged and bumped his shins.

His mood grew feral, fueled by demon lust. "I know why."

She nodded then stopped. "Why what?"

"Why you're smoking as you are. I know the reason."

Color her surprised but mostly dismayed that he'd caught on to how threatened she felt by him and the others.

He shrugged. "I agree with what you want."

That didn't make sense unless he wasn't the prick she'd thought and was trying to be nice. If he was conceding victory and would follow her orders from now on, she couldn't have been happier. "Good."

"Yes. It will be." He slipped his arm around her waist and drew her into his solid chest, nothing but hard muscle.

Her skin tingled.

He ground his hips into hers. His cock blossomed against her cunt.

Zoe's spit dried up. She would have protested or asked him what the fuck he was doing but couldn't form words.

Stefin pressed her smoking tresses to his nose and inhaled deeply, his face dreamy. "How delightful." He made a lewd noise filled with lust. "I've never known another demon who flirted like this."

He'd lost her. She was light years past flirting, straight into reckless desire fueled by countless nights spent alone, unwanted and forgotten. Deprived to the point of madness, she wreathed her arms around his impossibly broad shoulders and snuggled into him. A purr quivered in her throat.

A sound she'd never made.

He grinned rakishly. "Now, you'll see who's boss."

"What?"

"Shhh." He swooped down.

His lips were silky and hot against hers, his stubble, oh, so masculine, scouring her skin. He pulled her close, held her tightly and speared his tongue into her mouth.

She sagged against him, adoring his sinfully rich scent and impressive bulk. It was no match for his decadent flavor that spoke of the depths of Hell, sinful nights and shameless need.

He plundered her mouth. His passion demanded she suck his tongue.

She did brazenly. Sounds poured through the room. A delicate whimper. A feminine moan. Noises a submissive makes.

Surely not from her.

Growling, Stefin deepened the kiss, cupped her ass and lifted her.

Unable to resist, she wrapped her legs around his lean hips and enjoyed herself as she hadn't in years, or ever really. She drove her fingers through his thick, silky hair and rubbed her small boobs against his chest.

He staggered back but didn't pull his mouth free.

She would have bitched if he had.

Groaning like the undead, Stefin angled his head for better penetration, filled her mouth even more with his tongue and carried her from the room.

A piercing shriek tore down the hall, joined by loud thumps, curses and a lusty wail.

Zoe wasn't certain whether she'd made the last sound. Breathing as well as she could, given how Stefin had welded their lips together, she dove in for more and pushed his tongue aside to shove hers into his mouth.

He stilled.

Maybe he hadn't expected what she'd done since he seemed on the medieval side when it came to how a woman should behave.

Too damn bad. Seizing the moment, she deepened her kiss.

A rumbling sound rushed from him, quivering his chest. He tightened his grip on her and opened a door.

Snapping teeth and growls poured from inside. Sounded like a were.

Zoe cupped Stefin's face and practically devoured his mouth.

He opened the next door he reached.

"Hey." A staffer snarled. "We're busy here."

Someone, or rather something, shrieked. The door slammed, blocking the racket.

Other sounds intruded, mingling with the noise from Zoe's sloppy kiss. Her carnal skills were artless, but she couldn't help it. She hadn't had much practice and wanted to make up for that now. She dug her fingers into Stefin's skull to keep him close, his mouth on hers.

He opened another door and staggered inside the empty treatment room, his breathing rough, hands roaming. He fondled her boob, cupped her ass and explored the furrow between her cheeks.

Forgotten delight raced through Zoe and settled in her cunt. She needed more of this even as good sense demanded she stop.

Stefin put her on her feet.

She hadn't wanted that.

He glanced at Taro and Anatol, who'd followed them inside. Taro swung the door closed and stepped closer. So did Anatol.

Zoe couldn't catch her breath.

They surrounded her, each a mountain of a man. Completely irresistible.

The room listed. Their sulfur and musk scents thickened the air.

Stefin undressed quite casually, the human way, one button at a time.

There seemed to be a zillion, the V in his shirt opening slowly. Watching this was like waiting to open a gift on S&M Day, which stood for Satan and Me, the most sacred holiday in Hell, the presents way badder than a mortal would get at Christmas.

Tats covered Stefin's impressive torso and arms, many in a language she didn't know. A stylized goat's head decorated his left hand.

The Devil's mark.

She couldn't deny the image was exciting, the same as his slow striptease. However, it was against office rules for any staffer to undress during work.

Anatol and Taro watched Stefin a split-second, exchanged a glance then tossed their boots, socks, slacks and shirts until each was down to his stretchy boxer briefs. Anatol's were dark gray, Taro's navy, Stefin's black, the bulges between their legs ginormous.

Perspiration ran down her back.

They peeled off their underwear. Their cocks were hard, proud and pointing at her from hairy groins. Their curls as she'd envisioned — thick and fragrant in blond, black and auburn. Short hairs dusted their fleshy balls, rounded and firm with need. Prominent veins snaked up their erect shafts, the heads lust swollen and dark from desire. Pre-cum glistened on their tiny slits.

Zoe wanted to taste them so badly she would have given her soul to do so but couldn't. She'd already sold the stupid thing to get her first guy, who hadn't been impressed.

Given that history, she shouldn't be in here alone with these three.

On its own, the treatment table transformed into a four-poster bed, big enough for her and the guys. Manacles, chains, ropes, whips and riding crops hung from the wooden columns and swayed hypnotically.

She blinked and shook her head. "Hold it...stop." Her breathless command made her sound turned on rather than shocked. She chided herself and got tough. "What in the hell is that?" She pointed at the mattress.

"Our special place." Stefin stared at her heaving breasts. "You told us not to get comfortable in the other room. So I found this one."

He'd lost his friggin' mind.

"However, with you way over there and us way over here, nothing can happen. We need to fix that." Grinning playfully, he gestured her closer and pointed at his feet.

Like a Master would. A man who'd take what he wanted and would deliver exquisite satisfaction, making her cry out from the punishment, shriek joyously at the pleasure and shiver from her release.

Fighting her arousal, Zoe crossed her arms. "Here's a newsflash. This isn't the fourth century. You can't behave like Neanderthals in this place."

The guys exchanged a glance.

Anatol's mouth turned down. "Surely, you're not including me in that, *chérie*." He wiggled his eyebrows. "I know how to treat a woman."

His shaft thickened.

Zoe ached. She longed. No sane woman or female demon could deny how gorgeous he was. Romantic, too. His French accent was to die for, delightfully musical, its sound a sweet caress. He'd be a patient but ardent lover, until he took off and forgot about her, which he would.

She clenched her jaw.

Taro lifted his shoulders. "What's a Neanderthal?"

"What you are." Anatol took in Taro and shook his head. "Clueless and vulgar."

"Wrong." Zoe pinned them with her gaze. "It's a subhuman that strutted around naked. Like you guys." She tried not to drool over their sculptured abs and pecs, their muscular legs and hair-roughened skin. "The fact that a Neanderthal is also simpleminded and coarse is a coincidence. Get dressed. All of you. We're not here to play."

Stefin made a face. "Then why are you behaving as you are?"

Totally lost, she took a wild guess. "You mean acting liked a professional?"

"No. From the moment we arrived, you've been coming on to us."

"In what universe?"

"There." He pointed at her smoky hair and shoulders. "You're doing it again. That's how you flirt." He inhaled deeply and moaned. "I like it."

He was undeniably beautiful but fucking dense when it came to women. "I'm irritated." Her embarrassment had gone poof when they'd stripped. "That's why I'm smoking. Let that be a warning to each of you in the future. You'll do what I say when I say it."

Anatol and Taro stroked their cocks, making them thicker and longer. Stefin crossed his arms over his chest. The way a Master would when he expected a submissive to fall to her knees and tend his rod.

Zoe was sorely tempted but stood her ground. "Just so you know, there are laws against workplace and sexual harassment. They're posted in the break room. I trust you all can read?"

"We don't need to." Stefin arched one eyebrow. "You're the one who's harassing us."

"What?"

He sighed loudly. "You're trying to deny what's rightfully ours."

"Oh that. Sorry. Didn't know you were nudists. Does Becca know?"

Anatol sniggered.

Stefin threw him a frown and gave Zoe a mischievous look. "You know exactly what I mean."

"'Fraid not. Maybe you should spell it out."

"Very well. From this moment forward, you're working for us as a female should, and as I know you truly want, no matter how obstinate you pretend to be. That's merely a game. Nice, but not necessary." He tightened his arms against his chest. His massive biceps strained and his tats danced. "You'll do whatever we demand, including taking care of our carnal needs. Trust me, there are many." His nostrils flared slightly. "We call the shots, not you. We're in command, not you. I suspect you already know how simply perfect that will be."

He looked like he really believed that crap. "Seriously?"

Stefin wagged a finger. "You're not supposed to question what I say."

"You mean waste words on you? I wouldn't think of it." She flung out her hand and released pent-up power she'd promised never to use again.

A thunderous crack ripped through the room. Light blazed.

Zoe landed in the hall. Taro, Anatol and Stefin were locked inside the room. Hopefully for good.

It was Stefin's damn fault. She'd tried to be reasonable, as Becca wanted, and where had that behavior gotten her? Him saying she was going to be his office and sex slave.

The last part sounded exciting, but wasn't happening.

Constance entered the hall and stopped mid-step, her full-length gown swishing around her legs. The dusty-rose fabric matched her turban and complemented her ebony complexion. She stared at Zoe then circled her slowly.

Zoe turned at the same time Constance did.

They spun in place.

Dizzy, Zoe stopped. "What?"

"I might ask you that. What happened to your clothes?"

Her blouse was unbuttoned to the waist and the tails hung out. She couldn't recall when that had happened. Her unfastened skirt had fallen to her thighs.

Swearing, she buttoned, zipped and smoothed her clothes until she was back to her old self, pissed and smoking away.

Constance regarded the treatment room. The old door was gone, replaced by a thick steel one, the kind used for a bank vault or a morgue, to keep stuff inside. "Who, or what, is in there?"

"Pricks."

She eyed Zoe's outfit and her mouth.

Her lips felt twice their usual size thanks to Stefin's hard and ruthless kiss. Passion that went so deep she could still taste him on her tongue. Her pussy couldn't have gotten wetter, or her soft folds plumper.

Constance tapped her bejeweled finger against her cheek and smiled conspiratorially. "Someone's been bad."

Zoe stepped back. "They started it."

"They?"

"I don't want to talk about it." She pivoted and strode down the hall.

Constance caught up, grabbed Zoe's arm and dragged her back. "Ah, hon, you can't leave them in there forever. By the way, how many are we discussing here? What are they exactly? Vamps? Weres? Satyrs? Zombies?"

"SOBs. Three of them, all right?"

"If you say so." She lifted her hands. "I'll just remove those nasty memories from you, and you'll be as good as new."

Zoe dashed back so quickly her butt hit the wall. "Don't touch my head or one freaking memory."

Constance offered a knowing look. "Wouldn't think of it. Those pricks must be something if you want to remember them that badly."

She sagged. "Even you couldn't erase the stuff they just did." Those memories were burned into her mind for eternity. Hopefully, they would keep her company during her barren nights.

"Oh, yeah?" Constance bounced on her heels. "That good, huh?"

Freaking amazing and hopeless since their lust for her wouldn't last long. It never did with guys like that. This was about having their way, taking everything they could, including her pride then disappearing. Lots of luck with such an insane plan, since she wasn't playing.

"Come on." Constance squeezed Zoe's arm. "Tell me. Maybe I can help."

Wasn't likely, unless... Maybe Constance could remove their memories and they wouldn't recall having been here. They could go somewhere else and bother other female demons.

Zoe smiled then sobered at them wanting another woman. Of course, it was the most feasible way to get them out of her life before they did real damage. The only other option was hoping Constance could make this better. "Okay, maybe you can help."

"Absolutely. What happened?"

"First, he's all over me, then they strip, then he tells me I'm here to do his bidding in bed and out like everyone died and made him the freaking ruler of Heaven, Hell and Earth. Can you imagine?"

Interest sparkled in Constance's dark eyes. "Absolutely, I've had fantasies like that. He, or they, are real cavemen, huh?"

"He thought I was smoking to turn him on."

"Well, hey, as long as he's cute, it doesn't matter if he's not the brightest bulb in the pack."

"Try totally clueless when it comes to women."

Constance glanced at the door. "Maybe I can help get him on track."

More like in her bed. Jealousy slammed into Zoe. Dizzy, she fought to keep from growling. "Don't worry, you're never going to have to meet him or them."

Or remove their memories as she'd first considered. No matter what Becca might say, Zoe wasn't releasing Stefin, Taro and Anatol from the room for anything. They'd made her forget her promise never to use her powers again, to do things the mortal way and to suffer without love or sex as she had when she'd been alive. If she'd accepted her shitty life then she wouldn't have caved so easily to Satan. Now, she was back to square one, trying to be a good person. Dammit, Stefin, Anatol and Taro had killed her resolve and made her yearn. For that, they deserved to be locked up forever.

Constance screwed up her mouth. "You're sure about that?"

"Yeah—wait." She shook her head. "Sure about what?"

"Me never meeting them." She gestured to the steel door.

The metal was dissolving at a rapid rate.

Zoe threw up her hand and unleashed more pent-up power. White-hot light glared. When it faded, the steel was ten times as thick and protruded halfway into the hall.

Constance took it in. "Nice. Becca's never going to notice that."

Zoe stomped to her office.

* * * *

Anatol inclined his head to the door that was now so thick it had rammed the bed against the wall. "This is your fault, Stefin."

He didn't appreciate that accusation and slid his gaze to the man. "Mine?"

"Women need to be wooed. You should have used a little finesse."

Stefin leaned against the counter. "With one flick of my finger, I can send that door into the far reaches of the universe, but I haven't because Zoe would probably try to outdo my power, which she can't. Ever. When she calms down, I'll prove to her that she's no match for me. Something she should already know. Is that enough finesse for you?"

"Real smooth." Taro glanced around and used his power to lift the bed. His clothes were beneath it.

"However, what Anatol meant is to use finesse when you're speaking to Zoe."

Stefin thought back to what he'd said and didn't find anything wrong. "I told her the truth. Should I have lied?"

Anatol threw up his hands. "You should have wooed her first."

"How?"

"Sugarcoated it with some pretty words." In a blink, Taro was dressed, his power doing the work. "Not spit it all out like she's going to jump up and down, thrilled to death that you're going to be bossing her around." He wrinkled his nose. "Haven't you been near a woman before?"

Stefin clenched his jaw. "More than either of you will ever know through eternity. Remember, I was the only one who kissed her."

Taro pointed. "That's gonna change."

Anatol nodded.

Stefin recalled his and Zoe's kiss. Wild and wanton, yet soft and tender, too, bringing him back to his mortal days.

Having her in his arms had been nice. Given how she'd clung to him, Stefin would have thought he was saving her from Satan's more imaginative punishments. Like having to listen to a Justin Bieber album nonstop for twenty-four hours. Even the most depraved demons broke under that.

No matter how Zoe behaved now, she had returned his kiss, enjoying it and him. He hadn't forced her. She'd even pushed his tongue aside so she could taste his mouth, and he'd allowed it because he was a good guy. So much so, he believed women should have freedom.

Within reason.

Hadn't he granted her as much when he'd allowed her to drag her fingers through his hair, wrap her legs around his hips and grind her sweet little pussy against his aching cock?

Fucking A, he had. And Zoe had wanted him until she hadn't.

He couldn't figure out why. Maybe he should make this easy on them both and tell her that's why men ruled and women followed. No man could figure out what females really wanted and had to have.

Anatol twisted his dreadlocks into a ponytail that fell down his back. "Once Zoe's beneath me, she won't want anyone else."

Taro laughed. "She deserves better than you. I intend to be the first to mount her."

"Not if you don't know what pleases a woman." Anatol puffed out his chest. "I'll have to show you how that works."

Neither demon would have Zoe first. They'd all take her at once, something Stefin sensed she'd enjoy. He'd felt her building lust and tasted her escalating passion. She wanted them, and he wanted her. However, she wasn't a pushover despite her gender and size. As Anatol had said, they'd have to woo her first.

Now, all Stefin had to do was figure out how.

Chapter Three

Anatol sat to the right on Becca's sofa, Taro to the left. Stefin paced.

As far as Anatol was concerned, this was a complete waste of time. He knew how to make a woman respond the way a man wanted, but Stefin refused to listen, insisting on this meeting with Becca.

Her pained expression spoke volumes. "Did you guys fix the treatment room door?"

"Of course." Stefin waved his hand dismissively. "The door isn't the problem. Fixing Zoe is."

Becca frowned.

"Real smooth." Taro shook his head.

"Let me explain what these two fools can't." Anatol leaned forward, elbows on his knees, hands clasped to show his sincere concern. The attitude women needed from a man, even if he didn't mean anything he said. A barbarian like Stefin would have understood such matters if he paid attention to something other than his overinflated opinion of himself. "We want to make certain Zoe's happy."

She was a cute little thing, scrappy as all get out. Already Anatol liked her. He smiled.

Stefin's mood was downright grim, lips pressed into a hard line, eyebrows drawn together. "Happy, yes, but in the sense of being obedient to me. You know, taking orders gracefully, submitting instantly with no lip whatsoever or going ballistic with her futile power displays. I want her to enjoy serving a male superior in all ways as a female should." He halted and spoke to Becca. "How do I get her to do that?"

She made a face. "Are you serious?"

"Unfortunately, he is." Anatol affected his most exasperated look to show he agreed with Becca's distaste for what Stefin had said, another way to ensure a female's trust. "I've tried to explain that one, he's not in charge here, and two, a woman needs to be treated carefully in the beginning—wooed, if you will—to bring her to your side. In this case, it would be to our side, me, Taro and yes, even Stefin. Once that's accomplished, anything's possible and certainly easier for us to get precisely what we want."

She glared. "And. What. Do. You. Want? *Exactly*?"

Obedience, what else? In that, Stefin was on the money. Not that Anatol would state things so crudely. "I believe everyone will agree that there has to be order. A power structure, if you will. With men at the top."

"Uh-huh. I suppose females are at the bottom?"

"Not at all. Simply below men."

"I see. And are you saying you'd lie to Zoe to make that happen at work?"

"No, of course not." He frowned in offense, though he made the gesture mild to avoid putting Becca off. "I'd just tell her what she wants to hear to coax her to my way of thinking and what's right."

"Whether you mean what you say or not?"

Her clenched jaw bewildered Anatol. He pressed against the sofa. "No one can sincerely agree with another person all the time. Mild deceptions are a necessary evil."

She muttered something beneath her breath.

He didn't dare speak. Her snotty responses kept surprising him.

Taro scooted up on the cushion. "I told them they were nuts."

Anatol shot him a frown. "You have a better plan?"

"Hell, yeah. The only one that'll work. Never lie. All you have to do is sugarcoat whatever you're saying to a woman. Use pretty words so that's the only thing she hears and notices no matter what the hell else is going on, especially what's coming out of your mouth and what you're doing. Works like a charm every damn time."

Becca turned her outrage on him. "I don't advise you trying that with Zoe. She deserves better. Like honesty and respect. Ever hear of those two things?"

Stefin crossed his arms. "Are you saying she'll never be obedient to my will?"

Anatol held back a growl. "Have you heard nothing I've said?" A foolish question, but he was tired of Stefin trying to run the show. "It's not your will. No one died and made you king. It's *our* will. Nothing is going to change that."

"Think again. Since I'm so much bigger and stronger and more virile than you'll ever be, I call the shots in everything." He sniffed. "Just look at and listen to yourself. Talk about a sissy accent."

Anatol shot to his feet, his fists clenched to deliver an unearthly blow.

Becca stood. "Sit. Down."

Stefin growled. "How? I need to move. No chair, sofa or other furniture can hold back the power throbbing through me. It's vast and endless."

Anatol sneered.

Becca pointed at him. "You. Down. Now."

An obscenity rose to his throat. He pushed it back. "As you wish." Dutifully, he sank to the stiff cushion to show her he knew how to behave around a woman even if she was dead wrong. She should have begged him to turn Stefin into a roach and squash him beneath his shoe. Perhaps later, she'd come to her senses. "Despite how outrageously he behaves, I want to assure you that he, alone, will not be calling the shots with Zoe. We all will. We'll take turns. When we're finished with her, she'll treat us equally as her Masters. As things should be."

Stefin laughed derisively.

Becca tightened her jaw so hard, her neck muscles protruded.

Anatol couldn't blame her. Having to deal with Stefin was an ordeal.

"A little advice for all of you." She shoved her hair behind her ears. "Zoe will have your balls if she hears you talk like you have been. Don't expect me to stop her carnage. I'll be cheering her on."

"As well you should if we were to tell her what we said." Anatol smiled gently. "We have no intention of doing that. We'll mold her to our specifications, perhaps even using Taro's suggestion, without telling her what's actually happening."

"No, you won't. You're working together as a team. That includes her. The only one who's in charge here is me. So, behave yourselves. If you want to get along with Zoe, treat her like a human being. It's not that difficult."

He'd never been more confused. "I don't see how that's possible."

"Of course, you don't, but you had better figure it out and try."

Being a gentleman, he let her sarcasm pass. "How? We can't treat Zoe like a human being. She's a demon."

"You know what I mean." Becca gripped her desk. "Being a woman, I'm an authority on the subject. I know how we want to be treated by a guy."

"As you are with yours." He gestured to the photos on the cabinet behind her. "Your guy —"

"His name's Eric." Taro smacked Anatol's arm. "The one Daemon told us about."

"Yes, him." Stefin crossed to Becca's desk. "Daemon claimed he and Eric have the same feet. How's that possible? How do they get those suckers off and on again so they can share them?"

"Holy moly, they don't have the same ones." Taro gave Stefin a look that said he was insane. "They have the same kind. Daemon needed a pair to replace his hooves. Becca didn't know what potion to make so he ended up without feet until Heather had a meltdown —"

"Yes, yes." Stefin put up his hand for silence. "We already know Becca's a lousy witch."

She bared her teeth. "What?"

Taro ignored her. "In order to create Daemon's feet, she used Eric's as an example, even though they're ugly."

"They are not." She grabbed her smartphone. "I have a picture. They're beautiful."

"Please don't bother showing us." Anatol smiled patiently. "We've seen Daemon's feet. Horrible. So would you agree that when you say Eric's are beautiful that's a deception to make him feel good?"

Stefin leaned across the desk to her, his manner as threatening as a KGB agent. "And to get him to do what you want?"

"Move back." She spoke through her teeth. "Now."

He did.

"Zoe is not going to fall for BS, all right?" She gave them a hard stare. "If you want this to work, you're going to have to get to know her and grow a friendship. It's as simple as that."

Sounded like major effort and time to Anatol, when wooing was so much quicker, especially since Zoe hadn't resisted Stefin's kiss or anyone's nudity, at least at first. As he recalled, she'd been ready to rock and roll, which had certainly pleased him until she'd changed her mind. It appeared Stefin might be right about women not knowing the score, since Becca didn't seem to, either. "So we're supposed to get to know Zoe. Fine, I'm game. What's her story?"

"Her secrets particularly." Stefin grabbed a pen and pad from the desk. "Tell us. I'll write them down. We can use them to get her to do what we want."

"Not a chance." Becca snatched her stuff from him. "If you want to know about Zoe, ask her yourself. Better still, share something with her about your pasts. Be open, honest and vulnerable and mean what you say from the depths of your hearts and souls."

"We don't have any." Anatol wasn't certain why he had to keep pointing out the obvious to her. "We're demons."

Becca's face flushed dark red. "You. Know. What. I. Mean. Prove you can be hurt, too, and that your macho blustering is nothing more than an act to hide that you're not certain about things, either. You're no different than she is."

He tried to digest what she'd said and failed, hopelessly confused. "Wouldn't that be lying or even wooing to tell her we're the same, when we're not, or that we're as uncertain as she is when we aren't?"

Becca crossed her arms over her desk and lowered her head to them.

* * * *

Heavy footfalls sounded in the hall and stopped outside Zoe's office.

Zoe willed whoever it was to go away. They didn't. Reluctantly, she looked over.

Stefin, Anatol and Taro whispered frantically to each other.

She didn't want to know about what or how they'd escaped. *If they put one toe inside here...* Braced for battle, she concentrated on the file on her computer screen but couldn't read another word.

"No, no, no." Anatol sniffed. "My way is best."

Stefin offered a mocking laugh. "For what? Failure?"

"Both of you are dead wrong." Taro made a frustrated sound. "And beyond clueless."

She couldn't argue with that.

Their comments grew heated. Obscenities flew. Feet scuffled and thumps sounded on the walls.

As if they were fighting.

Couldn't be about who would have her first.

Outrage and desire washed over Zoe in equal measure. She could hardly forget how Stefin's kiss had melted her insides or the way Taro's and Anatol's cocks had stiffened when she'd stared at them, their male flesh drawing her near, thrilling her with their luscious rigidity and wicked good scents.

A rare and precious moment Stefin had destroyed when he'd admitted what they wanted from her — endless screwing and mindless submission, her doing all the work while they played.

The best sex in the universe couldn't make up for that crap. If they were arguing about who was going to tame her, they were in for a rude awakening.

She left her desk and stopped just inside her door. Smoke puffed from her hair.

Stefin and Taro faced each other in the hall like gunslingers from the old West. Flames flared in their eyes. They'd lifted their palms to release their power.

Anatol had one shoulder propped against the wall, his mood indifferent to the unfolding scene.

Smoke drifted from her to him. He batted at it and turned. His face lit up. "*Chérie.*"

Taro dropped his arm and looked over. Stefin gave her a wink and inched his palm higher.

She supposed to unleash his power on unsuspecting Taro. "Hold it right there." She pointed at Stefin.

He smiled seductively. "Would you care to take Taro's place?" Stefin rotated his hips. "We can have a very interesting battle between ourselves. I assure you, we'll both win."

The man was impossible. Drool worthy too, making her panties wet. "I shouldn't have used my powers before." She'd never forgive herself for that. "And I'm not calling on them again. Neither are any of you. Not while you're here. Got it?"

"I didn't use them when I undressed." Stefin gave her a sidelong glance. "I thought you'd like the mortal way better."

She had.

"Just a moment." Anatol waved his hands. "Why can't we use our powers?"

Her toes curled at his accent and rich skin, while those dreadlocks... If he grew those babies even longer, he could use them to bind her wrists, maybe even her ankles, making her vulnerable to his touch. Or not. She fought for composure.

Golden flames flickered in his eyes.

Those steady bobs captivated and drew her closer. The moth to the flame. She resisted and stepped back. "I don't believe in supernatural powers. I do everything the mortal way. It's one of my guiding principles."

A puzzled look crossed Taro's face. He rubbed his bristly chin, his gaze intent and on her.

Unnerved and aroused, she locked her knees to keep from throwing herself at him. "What?"

He smiled good-naturedly, a bit cautiously, too. "Not using your powers is kind of like carrying rocks on your back when you could use a wheelbarrow."

Now he questioned her good sense. She tapped her foot.

"Hey." He lifted his hands in surrender. "Just sayin'."

Stefin brushed past Taro. "Forgive him. He doesn't know how to talk to a woman."

Neither did Stefin. Zoe arched one eyebrow.

Her cynicism didn't register on his handsome face. "So you never use your powers and you have principles. Fascinating. Tell me everything about yourself. All of your secrets, good and bad, especially the bad." He looked intrigued. "I'll listen. I'll even agree with everything, just as you want."

Anatol lifted his face to the ceiling. "Imbecile."

Stefin threw him a murderous look. For her, his smile smoldered. "Come now, let's talk."

Zoe wasn't certain what to say. The flames in his eyes sputtered. Maybe that explained the sudden change in him from patronizing to merely self-absorbed. She spoke to the others, "Did the steel door whack him in the head when I made it bigger? Has he been acting strange, or stranger, ever since?"

Taro shook with laughter.

Stefin muttered what sounded like Russian obscenities. "I'm fine. We're supposed to talk. I'm supposed to listen."

"No." Anatol rubbed his forehead. "We're supposed to share."

Stefin's face went slack, his gaze thoughtful. He beamed. "You're right. I forgot that part." He faced Zoe, hung his head and clasped his hands. "Here's my story. I came from a poor Russian village. Times were terrible—the plagues, the scourges…you don't want to know." He sighed mournfully. "It's a miracle I survived as long as I did. I'm—"

"Full of it." Zoe swatted smoke away from her face. "I have your personnel file. The closest you've ever been to a Russian village is if Epcot has one at Disney World that I'm unaware of."

Stefin eyed her warily. "How can you be so certain where I've been? I told Becca nothing of my past."

Taro snickered. "Or the truth."

Stefin lifted his hand. A prelude to unleashing his power.

Typical. Men are such simple creatures. The ones she'd known during her brief mortal years and those since her damnation only thought about fighting, eating and sex. Not necessarily in that order. Love and commitment came last, if at all. "Rumble if you want. But remember, no supernatural powers."

Stefin reared back. "You might as well cut off my balls."

"Don't tempt me."

He took Zoe in as if he owned her, and had the right to strip her bare then bury his cock wherever he damn well pleased.

Her nipples tightened.

Stefin gave Taro the finger, crossed his arms and leaned down to her. "How could you know anything about me?"

"I got your file from Satan."

Anatol's eyebrows shot to his hairline. "You two are that tight?"

"Let's just say he prefers I'm here rather than there, so he caves whenever I want something in order to keep me from coming back." He'd begged her not to. She'd told him she'd think about it. After all, her free will sent her to Hell. It might as well come in handy for torturing him like he did her.

Stefin rubbed his chin. "You gave him a hard time, too, huh?"

"Not as much as you did with the poor communists. Wow, you guys in the Russian mafia don't fool around."

"You're right, we don't." He puffed out his chest. "Thanks."

Zoe was torn between sighing at how dense he was at times and kissing him breathless then ordering him and the others to strip for an examination. One she'd provide with her hands, mouth and tongue. Calling herself a fool, she battled her carnal urges. "That wasn't a compliment."

His eyes widened. The flames in them hid his irises. "You're insulting me because of my past? You want me to be ashamed of it? I did what I had to in order to survive. You know, eat, clothe myself, have a place to stay…"

For once, he wasn't putting on. Stefin hadn't gone into crime to enrich or amuse himself, though he had raised serious hell during that time. For once, Zoe couldn't blame him. He'd grown up in an impoverished household and was on his own at eleven, his father in a forced labor camp, even though Russia said they didn't have those any longer, his mother dead. Relatives refused to care for him. As a little boy without a home or family he'd had to become a man too quickly. Gangs, and later the mafia, were his only career choices. That was the info she'd been reading before coming out here. His tats were from the groups he'd joined, and from prison, too, telling his life story. Too bad she couldn't decipher the Russian symbols. She did know he'd cheated, lied, stole and intimidated, but he also treated the other gang members and those in the mafia like brothers, offering his life for theirs. They had mattered to him more than he did.

Tenderness flooded her when she didn't want it to, but there it was. She considered what he might have become if circumstances had been in his favor and he hadn't been forced to take the fast track to Hell.

He regarded her curiously. "What?"

"I'm sorry."

Delight glowed on his face. "Wonderful." He spoke to Anatol and Taro. "Sharing actually worked. Who would have thought?"

"Whoa." Zoe put up her hand before the others could answer. "What are you talking about?"

"Sharing." Stefin winked. "I told you my past and that made you sorry for how you behaved earlier. Now we can start at the beginning. I run the show with these two fools while you—"

Zoe pressed her fingers against his mouth to shut him up. His lips were so warm, his skin so bristly she wanted to moan but fought the urge. "I'm sorry you had a shitty childhood."

"S'okay." He kissed her palm.

Her hair stood on end. "I wasn't finished." She pulled her hand from his. "I'm also disturbed that you didn't learn anything from your past or being damned to Hell. By the way, how'd you escape your keepers down there to come here?"

Guilt flashed across his face. He shrugged it off. "Everything and everyone has a price or a limit. I did what I had to."

The shit he'd caused down there must have been major, given those blacked-out portions in his file. Satan had claimed the stuff was classified. Could be he hadn't wanted to alarm her and didn't want Stefin's return any more than he did hers.

Despite Stefin's caveman ways, Zoe felt close to him. They were both outcasts, always unwanted and unloved. "Do you want to talk about it?"

"Of course. I love to boast about my escapades."

Another answer like that and she'd be banging her head against the wall or shoving his into it. "I meant talk, share what happened and confess how wrong you were about whatever you did in your gangs and the mafia."

He stepped back. "I have no regrets."

Taro chuckled. "Wrong answer."

Zoe focused on him. "About you…"

Taro should have kept his big mouth shut, but, no, he had to lay on the sarcasm. Which shifted Zoe's indignation from Stefin to him.

Stefin smiled smugly.

Resigned to the inevitable, Taro caved. "What about me?"

"Your file had more portions blacked out than his." She jabbed her thumb in Stefin's direction. "What exactly did you do down there?"

He'd played cards with other demons to win their digs, ladies and whatever comforts they had that he coveted. No one could beat him at blackjack. If he'd lived during these times, he would have made a killing in Vegas and probably been whacked before he hightailed it out of town. Card counters were considered worse than mass murderers and bleeding-heart liberals to capitalists. There were plenty of plutocrats in Hell and they still had a bounty on him for beating the house too many times. He wasn't sorry about that. He'd made the best of a bad situation and avoided having to steal stuff, get caught then be subjected to the Bieb's shitty singing for hours on end as punishment. Any man, no matter how tough, would weep like a little girl when faced with that. However, Taro was also wise enough to know that he shouldn't boast about his bad behavior, at least not to Zoe. "What I did down there is nothing I'm proud of or that a lady should hear."

Her features softened. The smoke rising from her hair and shoulders thinned to a few wisps and disappeared.

Score one for him. Maybe now Anatol and Stefin would believe what he'd said, that sugarcoating things and using pretty words was the best way to reach a female.

Oddly enough, Taro wasn't proud of putting one over on Zoe. Wonder had blossomed on her face. She regarded him as one would a god who could stop time or create another universe. Like he was truly important, or he mattered to her.

Something inside him shifted. He recalled the ladies he'd bedded during his brief life before the sheriff shot him down in the street as he would a mangy dog. Robbing banks and churches usually ended like that for criminals, which is why he should have switched to gambling before he died. The girls he had slept with back then had had nothing but adoring smiles for him that had always collapsed beneath tears because he wouldn't settle down. He'd done nothing but take.

He sensed Zoe had experienced the same from the pricks she'd known.

Becca had said she deserved more than BS, and especially needed respect. Every being wanted that along with loyalty. Trusting a person certainly beat keeping one hand on a six-shooter, even in sleep, or having to zap someone from existence to come out ahead.

Rather than doing things the easy way, Zoe had opted for an impossibly hard journey. Although Taro thought she was nuts for choosing that path, deep down he admired her. "That wasn't true...what I just said." The words fell from his mouth before he could stop them.

Anatol groaned. "Idiot."

Misgiving flickered across Zoe's face, making her seem younger and more vulnerable. Her goofy piercings weren't Taro's style but didn't hide that she was a fine-looking woman. Her hair was so black it had blue highlights, her skin silky as satin and whiter than snow. She was sharp, too, and brave to have stood up to them. She deserved respect.

"I'm not ashamed of what I've done in the past." He hated to confess, but couldn't help himself. "Like Stefin, I had to survive. Granted, I took more than my share, but times were hard. I should have told you that from the outset. Fool that I am, I said what I did because it's what I thought you'd like to hear. All I wanted was to please you."

She got her dreamy look back that said his honesty was the best turn on ever.

Amazing. He wouldn't have guessed as much.

Stefin leaned toward Anatol. "Is telling her that also part of his act?"

Taro wanted to strangle Stefin.

Smoke rose from Zoe's right shoulder and hair.

He tried to reason. "What I just said and am saying now is not an act. It's the God's honest truth. I swear on my mother's grave." He'd never known her, but he hoped she'd been a fine person.

Zoe's distrust progressed to indifference.

For some reason, that hurt even worse. "I'm sorry if I've disappointed you."

"Don't be. We're not here to get chummy. This is the way things are going to work." She straightened to her full height. "I'm in charge of all of you, not the other way around. You do what I say. If you don't like it, you can go to Hell, literally. Or, if you want, I can have Constance lay her hands on your heads and remove every memory of your time here. We'll dump you someplace where you'll belong, let's say Wall Street or DC where all the crooks are. Your choice. If you want that, tell me now."

Stefin opened his mouth.

Anatol elbowed him hard before Stefin could bluster and make things worse.

No way was Taro going to speak. He'd already said too much by telling the truth. Something he hadn't done in nearly two centuries.

Look where it had gotten him.

Zoe jabbed her thumb at her office. "Inside."

Chapter Four

Taro, Stefin and Anatol remained rooted in place.

That pissed Zoe off royally, but she wasn't surprised they hadn't followed her orders. Like typical males, they had to come to a decision themselves after a female guided them in the right direction. Since she hated playing those games, she resigned herself to staying out there with them, even if they spent their entire existence in this spot.

Stefin blew out a breath. "Are you going to lock us up again?"

"There's a thought."

"*Chérie.*" Anatol smiled sweetly. "Becca won't like it if you mess up another door."

Zoe already knew that. She waited for Taro's two cents, most likely pure BS. His last lie had hurt to her core because she'd actually started to trust him.

He regarded her now the way a man would when no other woman existed.

Her brain turned to mush, her pussy ached and warning bells went off. He'd lied to her like a selfish bastard would, admitted as much and she still craved him. Shaken at her stupidity, she hardened herself against any emotion. "Behave and no one gets locked up."

Anatol nodded.

Stefin offered a cool look and followed Anatol inside.

Taro took up the rear, still quiet and watchful.

After gathering three pens and notepads, Zoe slapped a set in their hands. "Write down everything I say and commit it to memory."

Stefin clicked his pen and spoke softly to himself as he wrote. "Write down everything I say and — "

"Not that." She struggled not to laugh. "Only what's important."

He eyed her, embarrassment on his face.

Shame filled her faster than she would have believed or wanted. She hadn't meant to diminish him in any way. He wasn't stupid, just clueless when it came to social interaction, especially with a woman. "I'm sorry. I wasn't making fun. I'll tell you when to start writing."

He nodded curtly and lowered his pen and paper.

Zoe cleared her throat to hide how awful she felt. He was a proud demon. She figured he was used to women throwing themselves at his feet. Poor guy was going to freak out working under her command. Better prepare him for the worst. "Look at the walls in here."

Stefin and Anatol regarded them. They even twisted around to get a three-hundred-and-sixty-degree view.

Taro studied her, his blue eyes unearthly, so piercing they would have penetrated Zoe's soul if she'd had one.

Heat rose to her face. A lot more settled between her legs. "What?"

"I truly wasn't lying or putting on an act before when I 'fessed up about what I'd said. It's important to me that you believe that."

Stefin made a derisive noise.

She gestured for him to stop. Taro's admission might have just been words, but his eyes... Truth shone in them, brighter than the flames. Embarrassment for what he'd done softened his features and cracked the walls she'd built around herself. Again. Back and forth she went, not knowing how to feel. At this rate, he'd wear her out before the day ended. However, she couldn't push her renewed longing away. Warmth swept through her, making her deliciously weak.

Stefin waved his hand in her face.

She held back an oath. "What?"

"Shouldn't Taro be looking at your walls as Anatol and I are?"

How right he was. They had to get back to business. She gestured to her walls. "Look at them, not me."

Taro gazed at her for a moment longer before he glanced around.

She hauled in a deep breath and lost it at the awesome bulge behind his fly.

Stefin stepped between her and Taro, blocking her view.

She frowned.

He didn't back off.

Zoe should have minded, but didn't. He smelled delicious, pure sulfur and musk. She had to take a moment before she could trust her voice. "What do you see?"

Stefin twisted around. "Where?"

"On. The. Walls."

He looked then smacked his pen against the notepad. "It's not what we do see but what we don't." He pointed. "There aren't any claw marks in here like there are in the treatment rooms."

Anatol's face lit up. "That's right."

Stefin rocked on his heels as a Master might, his confidence and lust endless.

Zoe gripped her skirt before she touched his gorgeous mouth or more intimate parts, surprised she'd been ready to do so. Especially after what he'd said. "That's all you see in here, walls that don't have claw marks on them?"

He scanned the room once more.

Taro and Anatol did the same.

Each looked clueless.

She pinched her nose. "There are awards hanging on the walls."

Her awards that they hadn't noticed the last time they'd been in here. Ordinarily, Zoe wasn't one to brag. However, these guys needed to know she wasn't a lightweight.

Understanding flashed across Anatol's face. After reading the first one, he grinned over his shoulder at her. "You're a force to be reckoned with, huh?"

His praise and dreadlocks turned her inside out before she could resist. Although she'd never been a flirt, behaving like one now seemed right. "I thought you already knew that."

Stefin pushed Anatol aside to read the award and the others. "Impressive." His voice held new respect. "You would have done well in Russia with my comrades."

Zoe beamed. "I held my own in Hell, same as you. We surely gave Satan a run for his money, didn't we?"

They laughed.

Drifting from award to award, Taro scribbled furiously on his notepad.

Zoe joined him. "What are you doing?"

"Taking down what's important, just like you directed."

Her breath caught. For him to consider her awards special enough to record was... There weren't enough words to convey how he'd honored her.

She ached to hug him for his sweet regard, having experienced so little in the past from any man or demon. Wisely, though, she controlled herself. She didn't want him or the others to think a few kind words would allow them to put anything over on her. Although they were behaving now, that hardly meant she could trust them.

Time to prove why she was their boss.

The moment Taro finished documenting the last award, she strode to the door. "Follow me."

She wiggled her way down the hall, her skirt swaying provocatively.

Stefin wasn't certain he liked the new spring in her step.

He grabbed Taro's arm and kept his voice low. "Quit telling her what she wants to hear. You heard Becca. Be honest."

Taro pulled his arm away. "Who said I wasn't?"

"Me. Are you deaf?"

"Taro was being argumentative." Anatol passed them both.

Stefin caught up and assumed the lead as was his right. Having been the top badass in Hell, his position wasn't about to change here.

Zoe breezed into a treatment room. A tall, thin man squirmed on the table. His sunken eyes and ashen complexion resembled a corpse. His man bun didn't add any allure. So many leather restraints confined him, he looked like he was trying to emerge from a cocoon.

He hissed loudly at Zoe. His incisors elongated into fangs.

She swept her hand in the vamp's direction. "This is a client I restrained."

"Client?" He made a mocking noise. "More like prisoner. I've been cooling my heels for damn near three hours. No one has even walked by my door during that time no matter how hard I hollered. Where's my pissing attendant? Why the fucking long wait?"

"Quiet."

"Sure." He craned his neck and tried to bite her finger.

Stefin tensed, wanting to protect Zoe. No, he needed to, as a man should, and like she required, whether she was willing to admit it or not. At any other time, he would have flung the bastard to the far reaches of Hell for trying to harm her. Not wanting to make a wrong move or set her off, he kept his peace and waited.

"Write this down." She pointed at his pad.

He put pen to paper and scribbled as he spoke. "Write this down."

She pressed her fingers to her mouth but couldn't hide her smile.

Excitement flooded him. Her approval pleased Stefin more than he would have thought and convinced him he'd done the right thing by following her orders to the letter. It felt weird to surrender, but, hey, he was willing to try anything to get her to submit to him professionally and carnally. She was the boss for now, though that wouldn't last.

He gave her his softest smile.

Her lips parted and her gaze yielded as a woman's should when facing her Master. A man who'd dominate without cruelty and would possess without threat.

His balls and cock liked the notion. Both pressed against his fly to get to her.

The vamp snapped his teeth.

Startled, she looked over and frowned. "Bite me again, mister, and your days of sucking blood are over."

"That's why I'm in this godforsaken place." He struggled against his restraints. "To keep from doing that."

"Then use a little self-control, why don't you?"

"Wait." Stefin joined her. "Are you saying this thing actually bit you earlier?"

"Thing?" The vamp hissed.

"Quiet." Stefin spoke to Zoe. "Did he?"

She rested her hand against her neck. "I can take care of myself."

How brave she was. Foolish, too. "Were you hurt badly? Let me see."

Her blush reddened her face and throat. "It's okay, really."

"Show me. Please."

She dropped her hand.

Taro and Anatol pressed close. Stefin pushed them aside and tilted her chin so he could see her neck. Two puncture wounds surrounded by bruising marred her perfect flesh.

Outrage pumped through him.

"See, it wasn't so bad." She stepped back and bumped into the counter. "Actually, it's an occupational hazard. More for the vamps than for me. This one took a suck, gagged then bitched about how bad I tasted."

Stefin approached the vamp. "Is that true? You don't think she tastes as good as your other victims?"

The creature looked wary. He glanced from Stefin to Taro and Anatol then back. "She's a demon. I should have figured that out when I said hi and she got snippy. Is that any way to treat a paying customer? Not to mention, how she kept ordering me around. I was so busy trying to keep up, I didn't notice the flames in her eyes. Believe me if I had, I wouldn't have tried to suck her. Once I knew what she was, I let go fast. Not my fault she tasted like shit—ah, like hell. It's where she comes from."

"I agree."

The vamp brightened. "Seriously?"

"Of course. It isn't your fault how she tastes." Stefin tossed his notepad and pen on the counter and tightened his fists. "However, biting her falls completely on you."

The vamp shrank away as much as he could, which wasn't a lot, given his restraints.

If he hadn't already mortgaged his soul, Stefin would have exchanged it for the chance to use his powers. Unable to because of Zoe's directive, he pried the creature's lips apart and yanked out his right fang.

The vamp howled loud enough to shake the walls and furniture in here.

Zoe hollered over the noise. "What are you doing?"

"Making certain he can't bite you again." Stefin held out the bloody fang to her. "Hold this while I get the other one."

"Whoa, whoa, whoa." She bounced in place. "That's not the way we do things here."

Anatol and Taro wrote furiously on their notepads. Both shook their heads.

Their reactions clued Stefin in to the brutal truth. He'd fucked up again when he was merely trying to show Zoe the respect she needed and deserved. It seemed he'd never get this right.

The vamp wailed.

Stefin punched the table near his groin. "Quiet. Or I'll remove a part of you that really hurts."

The creature tried to draw his legs together. His restraints stopped him.

Stefin rolled the fang on his palm, his gift to Zoe that she didn't want. "Tell me how to put this back without my powers and I will."

She rushed to the door. "Heather!"

"Coming!" Her shout tore down the hall.

Heather bolted into the room, her pale hair and outfit swirling around her like a cloud. After skidding to a stop at Zoe's side, she gaped at the fang Stefin held. "Oh, no. How did that happen?"

"Never mind." Zoe rubbed her eyes. "Heal him, please."

"Of course." Heather took the tooth from Stefin and swallowed repeatedly, like she might hurl. She edged toward the vamp. "Easy, I won't hurt you."

He beat his fists and feet against the table. "I'm gonna sue all of you."

"Maybe I should call Constance." Heather looked at Zoe. "Get rid of his memories?"

"Later. Fix the tooth first."

"I'll hold him down for you." Stefin grabbed the vamp's neck and squeezed.

His eyes bulged but he didn't move.

Heather worked her magic, making both his fangs as deadly as they had been.

Stefin let go.

The vamp wheezed in air, tongued his teeth and snapped at her.

She jumped back.

Stefin frowned. "How come Heather gets to use her power, but I can't use mine?"

"Because she's good." Zoe stood on tiptoes and pushed her face into his. "You're not."

Their lips nearly touched. Her heated breath and intoxicating scent promised seduction and sin, nights spent in hedonistic pleasure. "You like that I'm bad. Don't tell me you don't."

Her hair stopped smoking.

Stefin hoped because her frustration had drained away.

It had. The flames in her eyes burned hot from passion and unfulfilled need.

None too soon for him. He pumped up the charm. "Let me give you what you really want and have to have." Him running the show. Her submitting effortlessly.

Offense replaced her passion.

Again, he'd read her wrong.

She brushed past him and spoke to Heather. "Get Constance."

The vamp squirmed. "I am so going to sue you maniacs."

"Fat chance." Zoe grabbed Stefin's notepad and pen. She slapped both against his chest. "Write down what you see in the next few minutes." She pointed at Taro and Anatol. "You too."

They gave Stefin a withering glance that said he was a cretin.

Fuming, he still managed to control himself. He was determined to play this game as Zoe wanted until she understood that his way wasn't only best but what she truly desired.

A strong man to show her the way to exquisite decadence and beyond.

A few more hours of this and Zoe figured she'd need a straitjacket to relax. Stefin, Anatol and Taro were supposed to make her work easier so she wouldn't kill herself even though she was already dead. What a huge laugh that was.

Constance strolled in.

The guys eyed her as they would a fresh soul dripping with innocence.

She wasn't any better and ogled them.

"No flirting." Zoe's jealousy fouled her mood even more. "Everyone get to work."

Heather zipped from the room to her desk. Anatol, Taro and Stefin lowered their faces to their notepads, but their gazes jumped back to Constance.

She raised her hands. "Just tell me what memories you want me to remove, sweetie, and they're gone."

"Not mine." She pushed Constance's hands away and pointed at the vamp. "His. Stefin yanked out his fang. Make him forget it and the long wait he's had."

The vamp tugged against his restraints. "No one better touch me again."

Ignoring him, Constance rested her hand on her chest and purred at Stefin. "You yanked out his fang all by yourself? Wow, you must be strong."

He grinned. "You can't imagine."

"I could try." Constance oozed lust. "If you're willing to show me how."

Zoe spoke to Taro and Anatol. "Don't write down what they're saying."

Their pens stopped moving across the paper.

Zoe pulled Constance away from the others and kept her voice down. "You're here for the vamp."

"I like our new staff members better."

She enjoyed any guys, mortal, immortal or otherwise. And they always noticed her more than they did Zoe. She hated how envious she felt but couldn't help it. Even though Stefin, Anatol and Taro were nutty and exasperating, she already craved them far too much. She pressed her mouth to Constance's ear. "Please. They're mine. Don't flirt with them or take them away from me. I can't compete with you."

Constance eased back then threw her arms around Zoe.

She tried to twist free. "Aw, hell, don't remove my memories of them."

"I'm not, so chill." She rubbed Zoe's back. "I was just being playful before. Don't worry, they're yours. I would never think to interfere in that. I couldn't. You're beautiful. You just don't see it like I do."

She lowered her face. "You need glasses."

"My eyesight's perfect." She swatted Zoe's ass. "Show those bad boys what you got. Take no prisoners. Enjoy yourself for a change." She released her.

"Wait." Zoe gripped Constance's wrist and spoke as softly as she had before. "I don't want MJ around them, either. I know I have no right to say that, but she's as great as you are in the looks department. There are tons of guys she can crawl all over other than the ones I like. Can you have a word with her?"

"Heather would probably be better for that. They're really tight."

"Yeah, but will she be able to threaten MJ if push comes to shove? I know it's wrong to be thinking along those lines, but…"

"Relax. I'll have a heart-to-heart with Heather. If she can't handle MJ, I swear I'll step in. I think a lot of what MJ does is put on. You know, for shock value. If chatting doesn't work, I'll ask Daemon to threaten her with solitary in his ring. Not that Heather would let him do it, but that should get the message across loud and clear. Back to work." She clasped the vamp's head.

He shrieked then calmed and glanced around the room. "What happened?" He frowned at Constance. "Who are you?"

She patted his shoulder. "The inspector who makes certain everything in this place meets all legal standards, mortal and supernatural." She looked at Zoe, her manner dead serious. "Your place passes again. From Crud to Stud has the best service and staff I've ever seen. I'm suggesting it and you for this year's award."

"Something else to put on your wall." Stefin bumped Zoe's arm. He gestured to Taro and Anatol. "Write that down."

As Stefin wrote on his notepad, Constance gave Zoe two thumbs-up and hurried from the room.

Finished with his entry, Stefin tapped his pen against his pad. "What's next?"

* * * *

Zoe felt as if she were in an episode of *Demon for the Day*, one of the most popular shows in Hell. Suddenly, Stefin, Anatol and Taro were eager to follow her orders…at least as much as they could. They were still green about the proper way to do things.

"Okay, tell me again, what are these?" She lifted two straps. "My right hand first then what's in my left — go."

"A leather restraint for normal cases and a titanium restraint for the problem ones." They'd chorused the answer.

"Very good." It had only taken them three tries to get it right. "And why do we use the titanium one?"

"So we don't have to call on our powers."

"Correct. And why shouldn't we do that?"

"It's wrong." Only Taro and Anatol had answered this time.

Zoe tapped her foot. "Stefin?"

"Yeah." He massaged his neck. "What they said."

"Remember that." She didn't want him backsliding and giving her grief. "Now what do we do if a client doesn't want us to confine him?" A trick question to see how they'd answer.

Anatol and Taro traded a glance.

Stefin made a fist. "Put the fear of God into the mother and make his putrid life flash before his beady little eyes." He relaxed his fingers. "Without our powers, of course."

"Not exactly." Leaving a client with broken bones, bruises and wounds that didn't bleed too badly was all right. Putting one into a permanent coma that Heather couldn't fix wasn't going to fly. "You use patience and skill." At this point, it was best for them to err on the gentle side, rather than use brute force. "I could try to explain further, but it's better for you guys to be hands on from here on out."

The vamp stared. "Are you talking about them doing that with me?"

She'd unfastened his restraints minutes ago and warned him not to budge. He hadn't, though now he squirmed. "Chill. Nothing bad is going to happen. Remember, the service is up for this year's award, like the inspector said, and I'll be here the entire time."

"Thanks, but I really feel I should get a discount on my treatment for this. I am helping you guys out, after all."

He wanted a freebie like everyone else. *Surprise, surprise.* "I'll talk to Becca. Taro." Zoe snapped her fingers. "You're up first."

Stefin stood in his way. "Why him and not me?"

"He took the most notes. Do that the next time, and you'll be up first."

He made a nasty sound but stepped back.

"Everyone watch Taro." She pointed at him. "You're on. Strap the client in so he can't attack anyone."

Taro cracked his knuckles and bunched his brawny shoulders.

"Ah, I've changed my mind." The vamp eyed the hall. "I'll come back when things aren't so busy here."

Taro caught him at the door, slung him over his shoulder and slammed him onto the table. It wasn't pretty, but it was effective and knocked out the vamp's breath. If there were bruises or broken bones, Heather could heal them later and add her service to the bill.

Once Taro had the vamp's arms and legs strapped in, he grabbed more restraints and wrapped them around the creature's mouth and head.

"No." Zoe grabbed Taro's forearm. His muscles hardened. Hers went weak. "That's too much."

He regarded his work "You're sure? He can't bite anyone now."

"Maybe not, but we don't do things that way around here. Go on." She pointed at the vamp. "Take those things off his head."

"If you say so." He whipped them away.

One end whapped the vamp's eye. He shouted.

"Easy." Zoe dug her nails into his shoulder. "You'll live. Good job, Taro."

He rocked on his heels. "My pleasure, ma'am."

She really liked his country-Western accent even though she hated the ma'am. Forgiving him for that faux pas, she returned his smile. "Please take off the restraints so we can continue the lesson. Anatol?" She motioned him over. "Once Taro is through, it's your turn."

"Him, too, before me?" Stefin fumed.

"Sorry, but he also took more notes." She pointed at Stefin's pad. "You might want to write that down for future reference."

He dug so hard into the paper she was surprised he didn't break the pen.

The vamp blinked wildly and shivered. "I really need to leave."

"In a sec." She backed away from Anatol. "Okay, do your thing."

"With pleasure, *chérie*."

The vamp screamed.

Anatol froze. "I haven't even touched him."

"Yeah, I know." She leaned against the counter. "We get skittish ones like this from time to time. Just ignore it."

"As you wish."

The vamp crawled up the wall to get away like a human fly. Anatol yanked him back to the table, secured him face down and shoved his notepad into the poor guy's mouth.

Zoe shook her head. "The gag is too much. It has to go."

Anatol pushed out his bottom lip like he wanted to argue, but shrugged instead and pulled the notebook out. "Better?"

His dimpled smile made everything awesome, even being damned. "Oh, yeah. That is, good job. Remember, we're here to help, not hurt."

The vamp grimaced. "Tell that to my attorney."

Zoe blocked the door. "Don't even think about running away. You've got one more staffer to practice with. Stefin, you're up, as soon as Anatol takes off the restraints."

As he did, Stefin regarded his notes and those the others made.

His concentration thrilled Zoe. At last, he was taking this and her seriously. "Ready? If you need more time..."

"No. I'm good to go."

The creature whimpered and cowered in the corner.

"On the table." Stefin flung his hand toward it. "Now. Keep me waiting and I'll blast you into so many pieces and to so many universes no one will ever be able to put you together again."

Zoe rubbed her neck. It was killing her. "No powers, remember?"

Stefin clenched his jaw, breathed hard and faced the vamp. "Forgive me. Get on the damn table or I'll break every bone in your fucking body."

"Better, but—"

"But what?" He gave her an exasperated look. "I did good. You just said so."

She wanted to smack and kiss him. "I know. But in order to heal all those injuries at this hour, Heather would have to log overtime. We can't add that to the bill. It wouldn't be right, which means the service would have to eat the added cost. Becca wouldn't like that. She wants to keep expenses down. Try again."

He shoved his hands through his hair.

His shirt stretched across his bod, his muscles tense, hard and totally male. The way they'd be if he plowed into her, his cock seeking her depths, his mouth imprisoning her tongue.

She gripped the counter for support. "Go on."

Stefin rotated his shoulders. They popped. Bliss crossed his face. "Screw this."

He clamped the vamp's throat, lifted him off his feet and dropped him on the table.

The vamp curled into a fetal position.

Stefin slapped on the restraints so quickly, he blurred. At last, he stepped back and gestured to his work.

The vamp's right foot was tied to his shoulder, his arms trapped against his chest, his eyes wild.

Stefin hooked his thumbs in his front pockets. "How's that?"

It was going to be a long night.

Chapter Five

Rough music boomed, booze flowed like water and ample fare covered every table at the Crucible, a New Orleans hot spot that catered to supernaturals.

Anatol sagged in his chair too tired to enjoy his wine and *boudin noir,* otherwise known as blood sausage to the less-than-genteel crowd. It was an urban myth that demons didn't eat or drink. Of course, they did. Hedonistic by nature, they would hardly forgo such human pleasure unless they hadn't enough energy to chew, much less swallow. "If I never see another vamp again, it will be too soon."

A different waitress from their last approached the table. She swatted at the thick smoke that hung over this place like a toxic cloud, courtesy of cigars, cigarettes and possibly demons like Zoe. Reaching them, she licked her fangs.

Stefin elbowed Anatol. "Looks like you're getting your wish. Or not getting it, as the case may be."

Anatol smiled faintly at the vamp.

Stefin threw back his head and downed another vodka shot.

She regarded his nearly finished borscht, a gross mixture boasting beetroot, potatoes and sour cream. As revolting and barbaric as he was. She gestured to the swill. "Another bowl?"

He belched.

Grinning, she eyed the tat on his hand.

Stefin cupped her ass and fondled her cheeks roughly. "I'm good."

"Hmm. I'll say."

She had to be angling for a good tip. Stefin was crude to the extreme, not to mention an excruciatingly slow study on how to handle clients at the service. That's why he, Anatol and Taro had spent forever restraining the damn vamp until Zoe had declared their work sufficient, after which she'd made them write an essay on what they'd learned.

Anatol had finished first. Stefin had come in last, of course, making everyone wait until he was done. He'd illustrated his work with X-rated images of himself.

For that, Zoe had deducted several points and made him redo it without the drawings.

Through it all, Anatol had maintained his patience. Surprisingly, Stefin had, too. Taro had been the same. Even choirboys weren't as docile. Anatol had expected her to offer a small reward for their efforts. For him, her mouth on his cock, his tongue on her clit or even vanilla sex, missionary-style. Starvation rations when it came to a demon, but better than nothing.

That's what they'd gotten—zero, zip, nada. She'd kept her clothes on, ordered them to study their notes in preparation for their next shift then left the treatment room without a backward glance.

The waitress grabbed Taro's hair and lifted his head from the table. "Is he okay?"

Hard to tell when it came to him. Although he was nearly as uncouth as Stefin, he was far quieter. "I'm guessing he's tired."

She released him. His face clunked against the wood. His arms hung loosely at his sides. She smiled conspiratorially. "You bad boys been harvesting souls, huh?"

That would have been a picnic. When Satan had ordered Anatol to take this gig, it'd sounded like fun. Not once had he suspected he'd be working with Zoe, or rather, for her. No way was she going to relinquish her command to them. As she'd barked orders, the flames in her eyes had burned brightly. Excitement had flushed her complexion. Her enchanting fragrance had intensified.

The sulfur-and-musk scent had made him damn near drunk with need.

She'd known. Desire had mounted in her eyes that she'd fought even though he and the others had done every freaking thing she'd asked.

Stefin murmured something to the waitress.

She giggled then rapped her knuckles against their table. "Holler if you need anything else."

Anatol certainly did, starting with another longing gaze from Zoe. Similar to the few she'd given him this evening. A smile would have been nice, too. Wild monkey sex would have been better than anything else. Not that he'd get it. "This can't go on."

Stefin held up his nearly empty vodka bottle. "You're right. I need another liter."

Anatol pulled Stefin's arm down before he could signal the waitress. "I meant with Zoe. Pay attention. Get with the program."

Stefin pulled free. "What program is that? The one where you have all the answers when it comes to her?" He pushed his face into Anatol's. "Or is that your precious *finesse*?" Stefin eased back. "How's that working for you?"

The doomed souls who populated the worst circles in Hell were doing better than Anatol was.

His rod was so hard his skin was in danger of splitting. His balls needed to shoot their load into Zoe's sweet pussy. Of course, there were ample females here to see to his needs, many dressed to thrill in leather or Spandex. Both materials hugged their bountiful curves.

Somehow, those outfits didn't compare to Zoe's long plaid skirt, prim blouse, anklet socks and saddle oxfords. Anatol didn't understand his sudden fetish for that stuff, unless the real allure was Zoe, a demon like no other, her ridiculous morals not quite masking the simmering sensuality underneath. Damn it all, her principles heightened her appeal.

Just as Gigi's had so long ago. She was the only woman Anatol had ever loved when he'd been alive, even wanting to change his bad-boy ways for her. They'd met when she was still in *lycée*, what the French called high school. He'd been thrown out for numerous violations from missing classes, engaging in fights, gambling and being a general dick. Not that he'd cared. School was for fools…until she'd come along. Her beauty had captured his attention first. Her morals had intrigued him. No matter how he'd wooed, she hadn't succumbed to what he'd considered his dynamite charms. He'd finally asked what he could do to gain one date with her. She'd told him she wanted an educated man.

Given his reputation, no school would take him on. She might as well have asked him to fly without a plane to prove his devotion. Rather than giving up, he'd hired tutors and paid them with money he'd stolen. Not that he'd told her as much. Gradually, he'd grown to like learning. They'd studied together. She'd graduated and so had he. Their love had blossomed, as had his future. He'd planned to be a playwright. Gigi had wanted to study costume design. Giddy with youth and hope, they'd laid out their futures. The war had ended their dreams, taking her during an Allied bombing. He'd gone crazy from grief, dismissed ethics as so much nonsense and sought nothing except survival and pleasure.

That decision had landed him in Hell. The last he'd heard, she was in Heaven and had hooked up with a guy who had a PhD in literature. Together, they put on plays for their fellow angels.

The memory should have hurt, but time and now Zoe had taken away the sting.

He frowned at Stefin. "We did everything she asked. Admittedly, we did it wrong at first, especially you, but we gave it our all and finally met her standards." He threw up his hands. "She should be here with us, on our table, literally."

On either side, demons and weres hit home runs with their ladies, babes nude as the day they'd been born. Spread-eagle, they wailed in ecstasy. Their dates or significant others made crude noises and licked, sucked or screwed them.

"Fuck this." Stefin pulled out his smartphone.

"You're going to call Zoe?" Anatol couldn't believe he was going to demand she come here. No way would she drag her cute little butt to this place just because Stefin ordered her to do so. She'd probably make their existence worse than Hell because he'd crossed another line with her. "Do yourself and me a favor. Don't contact her. Ever."

Stefin yanked his phone from Anatol's grasp and brought the instrument to his ear. "I'm not calling her. I've rung up— Becca, hey." He straightened. "Stefin here. I have a question about Zoe. Earlier you said we needed to grow a friendship with her to make this work. How long does that take exactly? Anatol, Taro and I are at the Crucible. Everyone's getting laid, except for us. Given how we slaved all night and then some, doing everything Zoe wanted, it's not fair for her to neglect our carnal needs. Even you must know that. So how many more hours will this friendship take before she breaks and caves to what we want, carnally and professionally?"

Despite those totally crass questions, Anatol held his breath and waited for Becca's answer.

Stefin made a face then lowered his phone.

Anatol slumped. "It's going to take that long?"

"What?"

"Did Becca say Zoe's transformation would be days or even weeks?" He hoped not months.

Stefin glared at his phone. "I'm changing service providers. The call dropped off before she'd uttered a word."

She'd hung up on him. Anatol wasn't surprised. "So we're back to square one with Zoe."

"Not entirely." Stefin shoved his phone in his pocket. "I know what I'm going to do from now on."

"What's that?"

He smiled broadly. "Let's wait to discuss it until Taro wakes up."

* * * *

During the next days, Zoe couldn't get over how compliant the guys had become. One might say uninterested, at least when it came to her.

On Halloween, they'd dressed up like Daemon, donning fake horns and tails for their costumes, even though their sulfur scent and flaming eyes gave them away as demons.

Although Zoe refused to participate in such a silly holiday, she did bring in her carrion flowers to show how to honor the supernatural world.

The guys stopped outside her office.

She used cardboard to fan the flower scent their way, a sure lure to reel in an oversexed demon.

Stefin looked over first. Taro and Anatol followed.

Feeling like a fool, she threw the cardboard across her office. "Damn fly. Shoo."

The guys departed without a word or even to ask whether she needed assistance with the nonexistent insect.

Later, they joined everyone in the break room. Heather wore a Wonder Woman costume. MJ's Egyptian priestess getup was short on fabric and long on skin.

Becca and Constance strolled in dressed as a witch and a voodoo priestess. What else? The sound system played that golden oldie *Monster Mash*.

Everyone danced, laughed and ate. No one noticed she was on the outside looking in.

She waited for MJ to make a move on the guys. Although she laughed with them and boogied on the table, she kept her hands to herself.

Heather or Daemon must have laid down the law to her. Not that it mattered. Taro, Stefin and Anatol never once glanced Zoe's way.

Tired of being ignored, she left. No one bothered to say goodbye. She doubted they'd noticed her departure.

The moment she dropped to her bed, she curled in a fetal position like the vamp had during Stefin's threats. Even in her darkest days when her first love had rejected her and she'd been bound for Hell, she'd never felt as alone.

Unfortunately, she had to get used to the emotion. Again.

She shouldn't have harbored hope that the guys would change and want her as is. Given that she was lightyears from beautiful, she'd need major magic or intensive plastic surgery to rise above plain. Her personality sucked. She didn't know how to flirt or loosen up and had never been what any man or demon had desired.

There was no way she could become a winner when she'd always failed. Her only choice was to accept what she was and soldier on in her craptastic existence.

The following day, she dragged into the office for her next shift.

Heather's smile wobbled. "Are you all right?"

Tears stung Zoe's eyes. She blinked them away. "Yeah, fine. Never been better."

"I'm glad. We missed you last night."

"Yeah?" Her spirits soared then went on autopilot. "Who missed me exactly?"

"Me, Becca, Constance and MJ."

Zoe didn't have the guts to ask about the guys.

Heather leaned up. "Why didn't you join us?"

"Halloween's not my thing. Talk to you later." Zoe plodded toward her office where she and Stefin had enjoyed their first and only kiss, going at it like real lovers. She passed the treatment room where he, Anatol and Taro had stripped. At the time, their thickened cocks had hungered for her. Precious moments that wouldn't happen again. They'd moved on, as all men did. Sorrow cut so deep it stole her breath. She sagged against the wall and lowered her head.

Footfalls sounded and stopped.

Not wanting to talk to anyone, Zoe turned into the wall and hid her face.

A zombie's groan floated from the next room. Joining it were a satyr's grunts and a were's curses.

The footfalls resumed then halted close to her.

No one had to tell Zoe it was Stefin. His unique scent was instantly recognizable.

A muffled belch sounded.

He must have just returned from a late lunch or an early dinner. She guessed some mystery meat dish buried beneath sour cream since that was his fave. Unless he was full from feasting on chocolate syrup slathered over a babe's pussy.

She rolled her aching forehead on the wall. "What?"

"I need a new notepad. This one's full." He pushed it in her face.

She backed away from the cruddy thing. Food smears and coffee cup rings decorated pornographic drawings that depicted him and a woman.

Stefin flipped past those pages.

There had to be twenty or more.

Zoe wanted to look at the drawings again. She could have sworn the naked woman had facial piercings, unless those marks were supposed to be zits or were food stains. Being a realist, she opted for the latter. A good-looking dude like Stefin wouldn't be drawing nude pictures of her.

She shuffled down the hall and gestured for him to follow. "This way."

He joined her in the storage closet.

The notepads should have been on the middle shelf not the top one. Since most everyone here was tall, they could easily reach them. Being short, she couldn't. Not only that, someone had taken the stepstool away.

She pushed to her toes and stretched as far as she could to reach the stack.

"Easy." Stefin stepped behind her. "I'll get it."

He pressed his rock-hard cock against her ass.

Shocking heat hit with the force of a two-by-four. Desire whizzed from her toes to her scalp. She sagged against the shelving, thankful for its support.

Stefin eased closer.

His scent washed over her, his strength and warmth more than she could resist. The pictures he'd drawn scrolled through her mind, fueled her lust and encouraged her to rip off his clothes to see what would happen.

She wiggled her ass into his groin and rigid shaft, the eighth wonder of the fucking world. Wanting more, she struggled to turn so she could snuggle her pussy against his rod.

He stepped back.

She looked over.

His gaze jerked from her ass. "Got it." He lifted the notepad. "Thanks." He pivoted and left the closet.

Panting, she sank to the floor and tried to figure out whether his behavior had been a blatant come-on or innocent because he didn't know his actions were inappropriate for an office. With Stefin she could never be sure.

She replayed the last seconds. The memory morphed into a triple X-rated fantasy—him lifting her skirt, yanking down her panties and plowing his cock into her channel all while shouting "I want you. I need you" in his thick accent.

Like that would ever happen.

Zoe pushed to her feet and smoothed her clothes. Rather than going to work, she searched for him.

He was at Heather's desk, discussing the appointments for tonight.

She waited for him to acknowledge her.

He didn't.

Zoe wanted to slug him but tramped toward a treatment room and the first client she needed to restrain. A were who required intense therapy before the weekend. He didn't want to call off his date with a mortal babe because the moon would be full.

Must be nice to have a guy make such a tender commitment.

She stomped into the room. "Yo. I'm…"

Anatol was already in here, looking hotter than sin, his black pants and shirt molded to his muscular form, dreadlocks skimming his shoulders. He gave her a bland smile, no dimple. However, flames flashed in his eyes.

Given their intensity, she would have jumped him in an instant if not for the were on the treatment table. The guy took her and Anatol in expectantly.

She guessed he was waiting for something to happen between them.

Fine with her. She closed the door.

Anatol approached, his stride as graceful as a panther's.

She forced down a swallow.

The were licked his lips.

Zoe couldn't blame him.

Anatol stopped. A breath or a kiss away. "Excuse me."

His mouth was so close their breaths mingled. Lust tore through her, brutal and wanting. "For what?" He hadn't done anything yet. She prayed he would.

He reached past her. His arm brushed her breast and his sigh glided across her skin, almost as arousing as a caress.

Her nipples peaked so fast they stung. Everything else on her softened. "Okay."

"Huh?"

Hell, she didn't know how to answer him or what was happening. Didn't he have a clue? "What are you doing?"

"I need to get the last restraint." He eased back and lifted the leather strap, the correct one for this generally pliant customer. "If you don't mind, Zoe."

She cared big time and ran his explanation around her brain. He needed a restraint and got it by copping a feel rather than asking her to move. Didn't add up. Felt good, though, except for him calling her Zoe, not *chérie.*

Tending the were, Anatol ignored her as if she wasn't in the room any longer. Exactly as Stefin had behaved earlier.

She leaned against the counter.

Anatol's pants hugged his firm ass and draped his powerful thighs. Every time he moved, his dreadlocks swayed, mesmerizing her.

For the second time this evening, she wasn't certain what had happened. Whether he'd brushed against her accidentally or accidentally on purpose. She couldn't figure out why he'd used her name, either. Zoe thought back to the previous days and tried to recall if he'd called her *chérie* then.

The memory eluded her.

Finished with the were, he strolled past. "Holler if you need me."

She wanted him to look at her.

He didn't, closing the door behind him.

The were smiled cautiously. "Is the treatment bad?"

He couldn't be serious. The way Anatol and Stefin had just behaved was far worse than anything she'd ever lived through. Having them ignore her on Halloween had been bad enough, but now they were kind of, sort of coming on to her then leaving her high and dry again.

Frowning, she left the room.

"Hey." The were whistled. "Wait."

She didn't.

He howled. "What about me? I don't have forever before the weekend."

Zoe didn't have time to get into that, she needed to find Taro and find out what the hell was going on. Of the three, Taro acted the most sincere. Could be she'd be able to bully him into telling her the truth—that they all wanted her, on their terms, so they were playing a game called hard to get.

It would certainly explain their behavior.

She checked the other treatment rooms. Taro wasn't in them when he should have been. Actually, he and Stefin were supposed to have accompanied Anatol, all three helping her strap in the were to continue their training…and so she could keep them close by.

Zoe hurried to the reception area.

Heather looked up and smiled guardedly. "Are you still feeling okay?"

She'd never been hornier or more confused. She propped her elbows on Heather's desk and leaned close to avoid anyone overhearing them. "When you and Daemon first hooked up, and you didn't want to get down and dirty with him because of your principles, did he play hard to get?"

Heather's face turned fifty shades of red. "Ah…"

"I don't mean to be nosy, but I gotta know."

"Why?" Heather leaned away from her. "Has Daemon said something?"

"Of course not. I just need to know if other men, that is men in general, ever act that way, playing hard to get in order to get what they want."

Heather sucked her bottom lip. "Daemon didn't have to. I was always jumping him. God, I'm so embarrassed." She covered her eyes.

So much for her helping. "How's MJ doing?" Zoe still worried about her. "She into any new guys?"

"Oh, yeah. She met several at Everything Goes. That's the club she, Daemon and I like. Lots of nice satyrs there. Nymphs, too. She's not into them, only the guys. Wait." Heather tapped her pen against her chin. "The club actually might be called Whatever Goes or So It Goes or—"

"Sounds like fun. So she's into those guys…at that club, whatever it's called…not anyone here?"

Heather's pale eyebrows lifted. She leaned close. "You mean Daemon? Absolutely not. The moment he met me, he stopped, ah…he didn't…that is, he and MJ don't—"

"That's cool. I'm glad for you. I was just wondering about workplace romances here."

"I don't think there are any except for Daemon and— oh, oh, oh, oh." She held up her hand. "I can't believe I forgot. Are you wondering what Constance talked to me about the other day?"

Zoe tried to act casual. She was so sweaty, her blouse stuck to her back. "Depends. Did it involve me?"

"Yeah." Heather cupped her mouth. "I told her I'd have a word with MJ. I did. She's not interested in your guys at all."

What a relief. "Hey, they're not my guys." Now that Zoe had a clear field, she needed to retain her dignity. "Any idea where Taro is?"

Heather pointed to the hall on the right.

"Which room?" There were at least a dozen.

"He was headed for your office to deliver your mail."

At any other time, Zoe would have rolled her eyes. Her mail was the circulars and other junk that came in with the real stuff. Heather always gave the discards to Zoe so she wouldn't feel left out since everyone else here got credit card offers, Victoria's Secret catalogs, promotions for life insurance…

To banks and retailers, a demon just didn't exist.

She hurried to her office.

Taro was inside, studying her awards. He turned and held her gaze.

The world spun.

He was beyond hot tonight, the overhead lights intensifying his auburn locks. His eyes were darker than she recalled, a fathomless blue, almost navy. She wanted to rub her cheeks against his stubble, eager to have it chafe her skin, and unleash the untamed demon beneath his civilized veneer.

He crossed to her.

Zoe's mouth went dry. A romantic movie filled her mind—him pulling her into his strong arms, ravaging her mouth and touching her every-freaking-where.

Taro stopped well short of her and the fantasy. He gestured to the junk mail he'd left on her desk. "Heather said that belonged to you."

"Why were you reading my awards?" She hoped that was his way of coming on to her.

He glanced at them. "I thought I'd written some of the stuff wrong in my notebook. I hadn't. Just wanted to make sure."

"Seriously?"

Arousal flickered across his handsome face.

Her pussy dampened.

He leaned close. "Do you mean am I lying?"

His scent was so divine she had to fight for control. "Are you?"

"Not always."

"What about now?"

"What do you think?"

Zoe laughed helplessly. "I don't know."

Taro looked past. "I have to get back to work."

She didn't budge. If he wanted to leave, he'd have to crawl over her.

His impassive demeanor gave nothing away. He edged past. The bulge behind his fly brushed her hip, his pecs skimmed her arm and his scent surrounded her.

As his footfalls faded, she hung on to the doorknob.

"Zoe." Becca motioned to her from the hall. "A client is waiting for you."

She'd forgotten about work. "On it."

In fast order, she manhandled a vamp and three other creatures who had booked services tonight. During each time, Stefin, Taro or Anatol provided additional muscle, but only because she insisted upon it. They performed admirably, for the most part. Somehow, they always managed to stand a little too close and brushed their various body parts against her.

She wouldn't have minded if desire hadn't been driving her freaking nuts, along with worry that they'd met someone outside this place to play with.

Twice, she'd wiggled her hips against theirs or pushed her ass into their thickened cocks because she couldn't concentrate on work and needed the physical contact. Finally, she'd had it and banished them from the room.

The newest client, a zombie, looked at her pleadingly.

She didn't have the strength to console him. Finished with strapping the poor slob in, she called down the hall to Heather. "I'm taking a break."

Heather smiled sweetly. "Have fun."

If it hadn't been against the rules, Zoe would have barricaded herself in her office and masturbated clear to the weekend. Unfortunately, a Milky Way and soda break would have to do.

She stormed to the break room and jerked to a stop.

Anatol, Stefin and Taro were at the table looking better than any demons had a right to. One million percent male, each in his prime.

So much pent-up desire rushed through her, she teetered.

The flames in their eyes blazed hotly.

Zoe knew what she wanted and it sure as hell wasn't food.

She stepped inside. "Fuck me."

Chapter Six

Stefin stood. Anatol and Taro followed. Their chairs slid away from them, propelled by an unseen force, the legs scraping the linoleum floor.

Zoe trembled.

Hands on his hips, Stefin lifted his chin. "On our terms."

His voice was lower than it had ever been. Straight from the depths of the underworld. The flames in his eyes flared, tempting her further.

She nodded. Hell, she surrendered.

The door slammed behind her.

The guys hadn't moved. Wasn't necessary. They'd used their evil powers to ensure privacy and were going to unleash their dark forces on her.

Zoe grinned, primed for this. She was well overdue, her pussy demanding satisfaction.

The air grew thick and electric. Energy crackled between her and them. Something brushed her. Felt like a thousand fingers. Faster than she could moan or blink, she was naked, her clothes discarded on a chair.

Stefin held her white cotton panties in his large hand.

Her cheeks burned, humiliation flooding her. She should have sported a thong tonight or gone bare-assed rather than wearing such virginal underwear only a grandmother would like. To have them see her nude in here wasn't much better. Unforgiving fluorescent lights accentuated her small boobs and skinny bod.

If they turned away in disappointment…

Their gazes raked her then lingered on her nipples and the dark, delicate curls between her legs.

Taro cracked a grin.

Anatol sighed blissfully.

Stefin pressed her panties to his face and inhaled. His lewd smile turned euphoric.

If she hadn't already fallen for them, she was a goner now. Moisture dampened her pussy. Her longing surged, becoming acute and painful.

Stefin growled like the demon and beast he was. His clothing evaporated. The garments reappeared neatly folded on the microwave.

Anatol's duds disappeared next. His stuff landed next to Stefin's.

Watchful as always, Taro got naked faster than the other two. His clothes materialized on the fridge.

As one, they faced her, their cocks rock hard and flushed from lust, their sacs weighty.

Fevered and wanting, she swayed.

Stefin pointed at his feet. A Master's command for his sexual slave to kneel before him and the others. To submit fully.

That should have snapped Zoe from her X-rated fog and stoked her indignation. Wasn't going to happen. She freaking loved this. It was a game, nothing more, them pretending to be in charge, her seeming to obey.

Meekly, she padded to Stefin, her steps unsteady. Intense desire battered her.

She dropped to her knees, her legs too weak to offer support.

Stefin's complexion turned a deep red. His lusty gaze owned her. He winked.

Everything went black.

Zoe couldn't see past whatever was wrapped around her head as a blindfold. Her wrists were bound tightly behind her. She suspected by her bra or socks.

This was amazing and getting better by the second.

The guys' feet slapped the floor. They padded around her.

She guessed to take in her nudity and submissive position. The next time this happened, if it did, she wanted them to record it so she could watch their moves during her breaks and after hours.

"Spread your legs wider. Now. Do not make us wait."

Taro's inflexible order made her skin sting. Her emotions see-sawed between embarrassment at her flawed body and anticipation at their crazed lust. She eased her knees apart. The coolish air licked her slick pussy.

"Not enough. Wider. Show us your cunt. How it fucking drips because it wants our cocks."

For a quiet guy, he knew how to bark a command. Wanting to please him and the others, she spread her legs as much as possible.

The guys were on the prowl again, circling her.

Someone thumbed her left nipple.

Her breath caught. She leaned into his touch.

He cupped her breast and fondled her roughly.

Had to be Stefin. He was the coarsest one, all demon.

Her head lolled on her shoulders. She yielded to her basest needs.

Another of the trio settled his mouth on her throat and sucked gently.

She craved more. His lips were unbelievably warm and satiny compared to his whiskered cheeks and chin. Zoe sensed it was Taro. He was the most sensitive, a complete wonder.

Hands spread her butt cheeks indecently and explored the furrow between them. She guessed Anatol. He paused on her anus and eased his finger into the tight ring, opening her for pleasure.

Nerve endings fired, leaving her breathless and sluggish.

She wouldn't have expected Anatol to behave so boldly. His impeccable manners and melodic accent made him too suave for this world. However, he was still a demon, one hundred percent bad boy.

Zoe ached for them to screw her raw and prove what Heaven really was. Certainly not a pie-in-the-sky place filled with uptight angels and syrupy harp music.

Someone lifted her chin. Musk wafted toward her. Unmistakably Stefin. The ultimate demon among the fallen.

He brushed his cock against her lips. The velvety head left a pre-cum trail.

Enraptured, she relished the taste, slightly salty and tinged with damnation. She parted her lips eagerly, fully engaged in this act, one that promised complete surrender and satisfied primitive need.

Inch by inch, Stefin slipped his rod into her mouth. He was a huge guy, decidedly blessed, his shaft ungodly long.

She swept her tongue over his thick length stiffened from passion and hotter than the lowest point in Hell. Determined to give him the best head he'd ever had, she encouraged him to burrow deeper.

He not only accommodated her — he fucking ruled.

Her nose brushed his thick, musky pelt. She reeled. This was too much for any woman, even a demon. Desiring far more, she fought her restraints, wanting to touch him.

Whatever held her wrists tightened considerably. A reminder she was there to serve.

Zoe did, her enthusiasm slavish. She glided her tongue over his hard shaft and flicked the bumpy skin behind his crown.

He yelled in Russian.

She'd found his uber-sensitive spot. Good for her. Smiling inwardly, she lapped it.

Rough noises poured from him.

She took his rigid cock to its root.

He pushed to his toes and dropped down, his heels smacking the floor. On an impatient growl, he cupped her head to keep her close and at her task.

Even a threat from Satan wouldn't get her to stop this. The only thing that could would be a crazy desire to tick Stefin off and see what would happen.

Zoe predicted he'd bind her wrists and ankles to a frame. A strap would dangle from his hand. His grin would be beyond wicked. He'd lick her ass good, marking and punishing her for being a bad, bad girl.

She sucked harder, her tongue frenzied, excitement egging her on.

Stefin stilled then bellowed loudly. His cum spurted into her mouth. Rich and thick, beyond heavenly.

She indulged in its wondrous taste and swallowed slowly to savor. Once she'd lapped his rod clean, she released him.

His crown hit her chin. Stumbling noises followed and furniture scraped the floor. He swore then panted.

Proof he'd had a great time. She'd never been as proud or realized how amazing a guy's desire could be.

Anatol pleasured her next, his musk as unique as Stefin's. Rather than accepting his cock, she turned her face away and licked his balls.

A strangled noise burst from him, so different than his lilting voice. This sound was rough and magnified his masculinity.

For the first time in forever, she felt exquisitely female. Her nipples were so hard they stung. Zoe welcomed the small hurt and craved more.

She eased Anatol's right nut into her mouth and delighted in its heat, his wrinkly skin roughened with hair. Tenderly, she sucked his ball.

His breaths quickened. He gripped her shoulders.

Either Stefin or Taro teased her tight ring, the strokes feathery.

Intense delight consumed her. She squirmed and whimpered but refused to release Anatol's ball or pause in her fervent attention to him. She licked, lapped and sucked.

He wheezed, unable to catch his breath.

She released him and tongued his other testicle into her mouth.

He yelled something in French.

Sounded like a curse, perhaps a prayer.

Didn't matter. It wouldn't save him from her lust. She worked him good and long then eased his crown between her lips.

He dripped pre-cum.

She couldn't have been more pleased and took in his full length, as she had Stefin's, and worked Anatol relentlessly.

He shuddered and blasted off on a pleasured roar.

His cum was slightly thicker than Stefin's, less creamy, but delicious, nonetheless.

His cock slipped from her mouth. He moved away, his feet slapping quick and hard. A loud thud followed.

She guessed he'd fallen against the counter. Hopefully, he hadn't hurt anything on himself.

Someone cupped her face and lifted it. Smelled like Taro. Willingly, she parted her lips to him. Rather than seek immediate relief as the others had, he kissed her forehead, nose and mouth. An intimate gesture that brought tears to her eyes and meant more than all the sweet talk in the world.

Thankfully, the blindfold hid her foolish emotions Taro wouldn't want to see. She knew how the world turned and what made guys tick. They worshipped sex, not commitment. A good time, not forever.

She'd given up that dream ages ago. Right now, the only thing that mattered was pleasure no matter how brief it lasted. She sought his cock eagerly, driven to give him his due. He was so erect his shaft could have penetrated steel, its scent the stuff of female dreams.

Zoe wallowed in his cock's rigidity and girth. Ropy veins dashed up the impressive column. She traced them with her tongue and slid his full length into her mouth. Her nose touched the thick pelt on his groin.

Ecstatic cries rushed from him.

She licked and sucked Taro mercilessly, taking no prisoners as Constance had advised.

Air hissed between his teeth. He drove his cock into Zoe's mouth, determined to run this show.

For now, it was his right as her Master, a privilege she'd given him and the others.

Stefin and Anatol played with her boobs, fondling gently and roughly, unable to settle on which they liked most.

She adored everything they did.

One touched her clit.

Pleasure shot everywhere. She breathed hard. Taro's scent filled her.

He enjoyed her at his leisure, his vigor pronounced.

Anatol and Stefin sucked her nipples. They stroked her clit and anus.

Ready to explode, she wiggled to get closer to them but also lapped Taro's cock, her enthusiasm unrestrained.

He wriggled, bounced and yelled raucously. "Damnation and hellfire!" His cum gushed into her mouth. "Aw, fuck, fuck, fuck!"

His drawl sounded cute and decidedly happy.

She licked his seed from his cock.

The bonds on her hands fell away. An invisible force pulled her wrists forward and secured them in front. Someone eased Zoe to her feet and lifted her into the air. She raised her chin to see beneath the blindfold. No dice. Footfalls rang from the right and left. A chair made skidding sounds on the floor.

She lay on the table, arms above her head, legs spread widely.

Hot breaths warmed her.

Stefin elbowed Anatol away and glared at Taro, warning them this feast belonged to him. To hell with everyone enjoying Zoe simultaneously. They already had. It was time for the main event.

For this, she's mine.

She'd honored him by taking his full cock inside her mouth, despite his exceptional size. Even Satan wasn't as long. The SOB could torture Stefin till time ended but he'd never admit anything else. To say he'd tickled Zoe's tonsils was an understatement. He was certain he'd gone deeper into her than any demon had before.

Oddly enough, those moments made him tender and playful now.

Rather than suck her nipples, he dragged his fingers across her palms.

She fisted her hands and tried to pull her wrists free. Her socks held fast. Harsh breaths quivered her pert little boobs.

Once he was through pleasuring her, she'd forget how to pull in air.

He leaned down until their lips nearly touched. "My terms, remember?"

Her vivid blush proved she did. Even so, she lifted her chin and struggled to see past her bra that blindfolded her.

"Uh-uh." He pressed closer, their mouths brushing against each other with his words. "Trying to see what's happening isn't allowed."

She made a face but arched her back, thrusting her breasts at him, and parted her legs widely.

That wasn't what he'd been referring to when he'd mentioned his terms. Not that it mattered. No fucking way would he pass up this opportunity. Her dark bush contrasted exquisitely against her pale skin, those delicate curls so damp from arousal he was going crazy.

He buried his face in her cunt.

Zoe pulled in a quick breath and wrapped her legs around his shoulders, keeping him to her.

Stefin couldn't have asked for better. He gloried in her womanly scent and the devilish fragrance beneath that spoke of brash need and endless lust. He licked her cleft and explored her soft folds, plump and damp.

On an impassioned groan, she dug her heels into his back.

No one had to tell him she wanted more.

He behaved as a Master would and worked two fingers into her sheath. Thankfully, she didn't bitch about that. If she'd yelled at him to stop, he would have been hard-pressed to do so. Her channel was stunningly narrow and strikingly hot, inflaming his desire to do everything he could with her. He rested his other hand on her precious stomach, drew her clit between his teeth and licked her lazily.

She wailed.

The racket she made cut off, muffed by Anatol's or Taro's tongue. Stefin wanted to send them to infinity and beyond for intruding in his domain but wasn't about to stop his own pleasure in order to do so. He ran his hand up Zoe's torso to her breast and collided with a bristly cheek.

Now, one had also claimed her nipple? Lousy fucking bastards. Rutting fools.

Possessiveness ate at Stefin as it had never done before. He pushed the feeling aside. He'd deal with Taro and Anatol later for daring to interfere in his pleasure with Zoe. For now, he concentrated on her response to him.

She twisted her hips at his zealous attention to her nub. Her sheath tightened around his fingers, signaling her impending orgasm.

Wasn't a chance in Hell he'd allow her to come this quickly.

She'd tied him in knots these last days, making him uncertain what to do to coax her into submission. His idea to alternately come on to then ignore her had worked. Not exactly the route Becca had advised him, Taro and Anatol to take, but she wasn't the one who was suffering. Sometimes a demon had to do what was necessary.

Stefin needed Zoe to understand his motivations and work for her release as she'd made him struggle to reach this moment. He slowed his licks and circled her nub rather than licking it. Ultimately forcing her to wait for pleasure and crave relief above anything else.

Anatol wasn't certain what Stefin was doing to Zoe's clit, but she moaned pitifully despite Taro's tongue being halfway down her throat.

Sounded like she was hurt or frustrated rather than turned on.

Anatol worried her hair and shoulders would start smoking again. Maybe catch fire and destroy the break room in a horrible blaze. In a flash, this could be history. They'd have to start over to woo her. *For the third or fourth time. Crap.*

Rather than worry about the coming conflagration, Stefin sucked her inner thigh.

Anatol couldn't believe it. Even though she was naked and spread-eagle on the table, Stefin was piddling around with stupid stuff. Anatol knew he should have gone down on her first since he had the most skill with women. Zoe had proved that when she'd sucked his balls, but didn't bother doing the same for the others. They hadn't deserved her attention as he had.

Chérie, I'm going to show you how a real demon gets it on.

He released her nipple and edged toward her cunt.

Stefin got there first. Without lifting his head, he punched Anatol, growled like a wild animal and really went at her.

Zoe wiggled like she was having a grand old time.

Torn between annihilating Stefin and seeing to her pleasure, Anatol settled on the latter. He latched on to her nipple and sucked for all he was worth. Although her bumpy areola and firm tip felt delightful against his tongue, to a demon this was still austerity rations and wouldn't satisfy for long.

Taro wanted more.

Zoe's kiss was better than he'd expected. Not only did he feel desired by her but cherished. A precious gift that made him crave everything she could give. Wasn't a soul alive or dead who could blame him.

I'm a grown man, a demon, for shit's sake, not an adolescent going to my first ice-cream social.

Frustrated from his building desire, he cupped Zoe's breast.

Anatol punched Taro's hand away and claimed her boob for himself.

Of all the… Despite Anatol's snobby ways and prissy speech, he was a greedy pig already sucking her other nipple. There were two of them, if he hadn't yet noticed. More than enough to share.

Taro bit back frustration and deepened his kiss, taking care with Zoe's piercings that pressed against his mouth. If this was all he was going to get for now, he was determined to capture her full attention again. Minutes before, their tongues had dueled, playing an intimate game to see if she'd fill his mouth or if he'd keep burrowing into hers. Stefin had done something that made her whine like crazy and concentrate on him instead.

She squirmed and tried to slide down the table to get closer to Stefin. He didn't stop her.

Bastard. Selfish prick.

Resolved to make her forget everyone but him, Taro kissed Zoe with tender care, his tongue and lips playful against hers.

She sighed breathily and slipped her tongue into his mouth.

He felt her victorious smile. Conceding defeat, he grinned in return and ran his thumb down her creamy throat.

She stiffened, pulled her mouth away and wailed like a banshee.

He froze, uncertain what he'd done.

Stefin grinned smugly, his lips shiny from her womanly moisture.

She shuddered from her climax.

"Screw finesse." Stefin gestured to her. "That's how it done."

Zoe gulped air and moaned loudly.

Taro curled his upper lip. "She hasn't had me yet."

Anatol crossed his arms. "Nor me."

Stefin kissed her inner thigh and grinned. "Who says she'll ever want either of you?"

The door to the break room flew open.

Taro couldn't believe Stefin hadn't locked and barricaded the damn thing. Even a moron would have considered that.

Becca regarded them.

Totally screwed, Taro held up his hands in surrender.

"Why'd you guys stop?" Zoe clawed the bra off her eyes and gaped at Becca.

Chapter Seven

As always, Zoe's bad luck was holding out. Unwilling to face the fallout any longer, she yanked her bra cups over her eyes. A dumb move, but it was all she had.

The cups didn't hide the entire break room. A sliver remained visible at the bottom. She lifted her head.

Becca stared at Taro, Anatol and Stefin.

No woman alive or dead could resist their awesomeness. Maybe their beastly magnetism would save them and her from a lecture, dismissal, protracted unemployment and the inevitable trip to a place worse than Hell since they were no longer welcomed there. Then again…

She wanted to curl into a ball and disappear.

Becca jabbed her thumb over her shoulder. "Out."

Stefin scratched his ass. His nearly erect cock bobbed with the movement. "This isn't what it seems."

His resonant voice sent heat trailing down Zoe's spine. Warmth curled in her belly.

Becca smiled cynically. "I'm sure." She inclined her head to the hall. "Out. Now. Get back to work."

Miracle of miracles, they still had jobs.

On a huff, Stefin padded to the door. His muscular ass flexed with each step.

"Whoa, whoa, whoa." Becca shook her head. "After you get dressed."

Anatol said something beneath his breath that sounded like "dimwit".

Stefin glared in his direction.

Sounds from rustling fabric filled the room. Fully clothed, he and the others strolled to the door.

Zoe couldn't believe it. After what she'd shared with them, including submitting like a braindead sub, they weren't going to use their powers to help her dress or even untie her hands. Typical freaking men. They'd gotten her naked, but hadn't been able to do the deed, so now they were history. Wasn't going to happen. She still called the shots around here. "Hey. What about me?"

They stopped and looked over. Anatol smiled hungrily, making a dimple. Raw lust tightened Stefin's features. Taro regarded Zoe's mouth, her boobs and cunt, desire in his eyes.

Okay, maybe she was ready to forgive them for being insensitive pricks.

Stefin spoke to Becca. "Zoe wants us to stay." He grinned. "Who can blame her?"

Becca shoved him and the others out of the door, closed and locked it.

Zoe sensed what was coming. The lecture no employee wanted to endure. She hung her head.

Silence pressed in.

If Becca expected a confession or an apology, she'd be waiting an eternity for it. Zoe wasn't sorry for doing what she had, only for having gotten caught. Next time, if there were a next time, she'd fortify the door with so much steel even Rowena's magic wouldn't get past it. Becca's shitty spells certainly couldn't.

She cleared her throat. "You okay?"

A curious question, considering. Zoe was naked and alone, the afterglow from her orgasms a distant memory. Of course, she wasn't all right. Too depressed to speak, she shrugged.

Becca gathered Zoe's things, put them on the table and undid the socks around her wrists. "I'm not mad, okay?"

She pushed the bra to her forehead. "You're not?"

"It's perfectly okay for you to have fun. I'd say you're well overdue, but not during business hours or on this table." She made a face. "The staff eats in here."

Zoe wasn't about to argue with such a legitimate consideration. However, she could hardly describe what had happened between her and the guys as mere fun, even if she'd initially let loose to relieve her sexual frustration.

Taro's tender kiss had changed her carnal hunger into something deeper, so had Anatol's response to her efforts in arousing him. Stefin's possessiveness had sent her over the edge. She'd heard him punching the others to keep them away so he could have her for himself.

No mortal or immortal guy had ever desired her so completely.

Whether their emotions were real or lasting was anyone's guess. She did know their zealous attention hadn't eased her loneliness and yearning for long. She was right back to where she'd started, possibly stuck in the same rut forever. Always wanting more. A forever after and the Cinderella fairytale. In her case starring three princes from the Dark Side.

Wasn't likely. She'd tried love once. Hadn't worked out. Could be having a good time was all she could expect.

Disillusioned and confused, she pulled her bra off her head. "I didn't mean for this to happen."

Becca nodded sympathetically.

Somehow, that made this worse than if she'd yelled. "That's not true. I told them to fuck me. It was either go for the gold or never have this."

She gestured to the hickey Stefin left on her inner thigh and the ones from Taro and Anatol on her boobs. Marks that proved lust, not tenderness, affection or love.

She was so screwed.

Becca patted Zoe's shoulder. "Happens to the best of us."

"Not to me. No one's ever wanted me before. I know I'm not much to look at, but I still have needs just like everyone else."

"Wait a sec. Not much to look at?" Becca cupped Zoe's chin. "Are you serious?"

"Do you see me laughing?" She crossed her arms over her meager breasts. "What's with you and Constance trying to make me believe I'm something special?"

"We're not trying. You are. No one in this universe is the same as you."

"Satan's certainly grateful for that."

Becca snickered then sobered. "So you like the guys, huh?"

"Who wouldn't?" She wanted to cry but didn't have the strength. "Have you ever seen cocks like that? And their balls, damn. Not to mention their gorgeous faces.

But that isn't the best part. Sure, they're hunks and I have to admit I like that, but deep, deep, deep down, they're good people. The crap they spew is pure bluster to puff themselves up like most men do. Basically, they're pussycats." She'd never been as weary. "No other guy in the universe will ever compare to them."

Becca propped her hip against the table. "I can think of one who does."

Eric, Becca's one and only. Admittedly, he was cute, but in a preppy way. Certainly not in the same league as Stefin, Anatol and Taro. Zoe had little choice except to lie and spare Becca's feelings. "You're right. He's a real hottie. You lucky dog."

Becca's face turned as red as her hair, making her one color. "Yeah, well, he's also lucky to have me."

"Of course. I didn't mean he wasn't."

"I know. What I'm trying to say is you have nothing to worry about when it comes to your appearance."

Swellings from bee stings were bigger than her breasts. Her legs were too short, her features unattractive, her complexion sallow. The best thing about her was her hair when it wasn't smoking.

Which it was, her frustration showing again. She swatted at the puffs.

Becca pulled a chair over and plopped into it. "Do you want to look different?"

Zoe leaned away. "I know you mean well, but I really don't want you to make a potion for me." Given Becca's hit-or-miss magic, Zoe figured she could end up looking like a female version of Dog the bounty hunter. That wasn't a chance she was willing to take, not even for romance. "I'm good as I am." She forced a smile. "I've lived with my imperfections for so long, at this point I can endure them for eternity."

Becca arched one flame-colored eyebrow. "I wasn't speaking of magic. More like a confidence booster. You know. A makeover."

"From me to what?"

"Quit downing yourself."

"I'm not. I'm being serious."

She rested her arms on the table. "A makeover that enhances your natural gifts. And don't you dare say you don't have any." She made a face. "Did the guys make a crack about how you look?"

"Why would they? Am I that awful?"

"No, no. Good Lord." She muttered something beneath her breath. "I was just wondering if they'd said anything to make you feel bad...or worse about yourself."

"We didn't talk that much."

Becca nodded knowingly. "Didn't they look at you as you wanted?"

Their intense gazes were one of the best parts of tonight. "Surprisingly, they stared a lot. But hey, even though the fluorescent lights revealed all my gory flaws, the guys didn't turn to stone."

"Will you stop talking like that?"

"Why? I know my shortcomings, okay? Sure, they were all over me, but they were horny. Who could blame them? You keep them cooped up here working the entire night. They need to blow off steam. I was here. I was available. I was—"

"Hoping for more?"

Zoe shrugged off the question, but endless yearning made her ache. "Not in the realm of possibility. There are tons of good-looking babes out there I can't compete with. A lot here too, including Constance and MJ."

"I don't think they're interested in the guys."

"Maybe they will be if I tell them it's okay. I probably should. That way it'd be like ripping off a scab while it's still yellow, soft and gooey to get rid of the pain that much faster."

Becca turned a little green. "Doing that will only deepen the hurt. Plus you'll have a new scab forming. No way you can get around that. It's basic science."

"I'm sure love and attraction work differently. Even if MJ and Constance don't want the guys, someone out there will. I can't compare to them."

"Who said you have to?" Becca held up her finger before Zoe could respond. "If the guys don't like you for you, you don't want them, because no matter how gorgeous, built, rich or wonderful you are, it will never be enough. They'll always be looking for someone new or different. You deserve better."

Of course, she did, but relationships had never worked out that way for her.

Rarely had she been as bewildered as now, especially given what Becca had said. "You really think I shouldn't change at all?"

"Are you comfortable with the way you are? Don't even consider what Anatol, Stefin and Taro might think. Concentrate on how you feel about yourself. Do you like your hair the way you wear it? Are you cool with your facial piercings? Are your clothes the kind you really like to wear?"

"How am I supposed to know? I was alive during the witch trials. Salem wasn't exactly known for its fashion sense."

"But what you saw in Hell was too crass?"

Night and day compared to what Zoe had known when she was alive. She'd been caught between two worlds for so long. Her prim clothes a product of her Puritan upbringing, her facial piercings a way to cut loose or to repel guys before they could reject her.

The truth struck so hard she bit her bottom lip to keep from crying out. Her tongue swept over her studs.

Becca studied her closely. "What?"

Zoe scooted off the table and yanked on her clothes. "Who'll be doing the makeover?"

"Ah, your choice. I can ask Heather, Constance and MJ to help, unless you object."

She'd be a fool if she did. Each was gorgeous, Constance and MJ's bods the stuff that populated every guy's wet dream. "Let's do it."

"Absolutely." Becca handed over Zoe's clothes. "Better get dressed first."

Once she had, they linked arms and entered the hall.

The guys were at the far end.

Under Stefin's imperious direction, Anatol and Taro half-escorted, half-dragged a reaper to a treatment room. He was butt-ugly, his pasty skin stretched tight over his skeletal face. Yellow teeth protruded past his thin lips.

Poor dude would need intense work for months if he wanted to resemble Brat Pitt in *Meet Joe Black*, every reaper's goal.

Becca pulled Zoe past the group.

She halted and turned around, tugging Becca with her.

"Sweetie." She shook Zoe's arm. "You're drooling."

Tell her something she didn't know. The guys were too luscious for her to do anything else.

"A little less obvious, okay?" Becca yanked her around. "You want them to come to you."

Sounded reasonable. Zoe figured she should behave as if she were certain of herself and the guys were lucky to have messed around with her. She was special. She was worthy.

She needed that makeover.

Stefin liked the hickey he'd left on Zoe's throat, proving his claim on her. He grinned.

Becca hurried Zoe down the hall and pushed her around the corner. Away from prying eyes.

He suspected she'd warned Zoe to steer clear of him, Taro and Anatol. At the very least to keep her clothes on during business hours.

What a killjoy.

He saw no harm in having enjoyed themselves. Zoe liked their play and wanted more. He would have given it to her too if they hadn't been rudely interrupted. Before that awful moment, her naked desire had snatched his breath and made his legs rubbery. A curious reaction for a demon who'd seen and experienced everything, but there it was. Zoe was beginning to affect him deeply.

Uncertain how to react, he stewed.

Anatol puffed. "A little help here?"

The reaper had dug his long nails into the doorjamb and held on to it for dear life.

Taro and Anatol struggled to pull him inside the mortal way. No powers.

The reaper moaned loud and long. "I've changed my mind."

Stefin didn't have time for this nonsense. "Too bad. You signed a contract."

"So fucking what?"

"Do you allow the dead to return to Earth just because they want to?"

"Are you nuts?" He bared his ugly teeth. "They can't go back, they're dead. Hell, they smell like shit because of it."

"You'll be worse than smelly and dead if you don't get your skinny ass in that room." Stefin wanted to get this over with and have the evening end so he and Zoe could continue what they'd started.

Taro and Anatol yanked. The jamb tore free from the frame.

Still clutching the splintered wood, the reaper howled.

They pulled him to the treatment table.

* * * *

Mistress Jin, MJ for short, leaned against her desk and studied Zoe as one would a specimen under a microscope. Not a particularly attractive one. Becca, Constance and Heather had already positioned their chairs to surround Zoe's. Possibly so she wouldn't run.

The urge to do so kept building. "Before we begin…"

"Yeah?" MJ leaned closer, her appeal pronounced, her looks otherworldly.

Zoe sagged. "Thanks for not going after my guys — that is, the guys. I appreciate it."

She flicked her wrist. The bells around them tinkled merrily. "No prob. They're not my type."

From what Zoe had witnessed here, every guy was, living or dead.

MJ shrugged. "I'm not their type, either."

That was a bald-faced lie. MJ's caramel-colored skin, violet eyes, waist-length black hair, curvalicious bod and exotic features were every man's fantasy. She even smelled decent. Her incense fragrance was decadent, sexy and mysterious. "I beg to differ. So thanks for keeping your hands off them. Really."

"You bet." She drummed her fingers. "Do you have any idea what you'd like to look like?"

Swallowing her pride, Zoe pointed at her. That's how she wanted to look.

"Exactly like me?"

She had to get real. There were losers in life so others could win. No one had to tell her what side of the fence she'd fallen on. "No. I mean, I don't want to look like you, not really. I don't want to look like anyone. I want to be me, only better."

Constance patted Zoe's knee. "Good answer."

At least it was politically correct for a modern, with-it woman. "I don't want to use magic, either." She shot a worried glance at Becca. Unless Rowena was willing to help out, no way would Zoe drink any potion Becca mixed, nor did she want spells hurled at her. "I want to do this the mortal way."

MJ's eyes widened. "That may take a while. What's the timeframe here?"

Zoe checked the wall clock. "The shift ends in four hours."

Becca scooted up. "You want to be made over so quickly?"

Sounded like that would be impossible when it came to her. Zoe frowned. "I thought you said I wasn't that bad."

"You're beautiful." Becca, Heather and Constance had spoken as one.

MJ nodded. "Nothing wrong with you, babe."

They were making her blush and feel more like an idiot than she already did. Zoe gestured to herself. "Absolutely nothing needs to be changed about me? I'm perfect?"

Becca squirmed. "Unique."

Constance nodded.

Heather averted her gaze. As a good fairy, she couldn't lie or sugarcoat stuff.

Zoe honed in on her like a heat-seeking missile. "What about you, Heather? Do you also think I'm unique, perfect and okay just as I am?"

She looked to the others for help. They gazed elsewhere. She slumped. "You, ah, you…"

Zoe leaned closer. "Go on. Spit it out. Now. Right this minute. Don't make me wait one more second for—"

"Okay, okay. You have a beautiful complexion. It's a shame to ruin it with the metal things." She slapped her hand over her mouth. "I shouldn't have said that. I'm so sorry. I didn't mean to be that blunt. Forgive me, please. I—"

"Not a problem." Zoe figured it was best to cut through the crap to reality. "Everyone else agree the metal's not attractive?"

They nodded.

"What about my clothes?"

MJ groaned, Constance made a face, Becca drew her finger across her neck in a slashing motion, Heather went into a full-body blush before offering a shaky thumbs-down.

Apparently, Zoe repelled women, as well as men. "So what now? Trust me, I'm too skinny to look good in Spandex or leather like other female demons."

MJ tapped her tapered nail against her cheek. "Let's see what we can do about what you have on."

Zoe pushed back in her chair. "If I don't like what you come up with, will I be able to take it off? You're not going to tattoo anything on me, are you?" She'd heard how MJ liked to screw around with people's wishes. When Daemon was still her Master, he'd asked for a Busch, as in beer. He'd gotten green leafy bushes instead. Ha-ha.

MJ cooed. "I'll be good."

Heather gave her an entreating look. "Promise?"

"Yep." She gestured to Zoe. "Stand up."

"Why?"

"Don't worry, it won't hurt. If it does, you can possess me and make my life shit. I'd totally deserve it."

Sounded like a plan. Zoe pushed to her feet.

Something popped.

Constance sucked in a breath.

Zoe froze.

She still had on her schoolgirl clothes, but the skirt was so short the hem barely reached her thighs. Her blouse couldn't have been tighter. She struggled to breathe, even though the garment was unbuttoned to beneath her breasts. Her bra peeked through. It wasn't snowy white any longer, but black and sequined. Padded, too, one of those Wonderbra things. Her anklet socks had morphed into lacy knee-highs, her saddle shoes replaced by Mary Janes, the heels four-inches.

Zoe wobbled. She grasped the chair to balance herself.

"Wow." Becca clutched her throat. "That's perfect for *Debbie does Delta Psi*."

"Exactly." Zoe glared at MJ. "I'm not starring in a porno flick or going trick or treating."

MJ offered a sly smile. "It'll be nothing except treats when you wear that, I can assure you."

"I think she'd prefer a subtler look." Heather smiled apologetically. "How about something in white?"

Constance flicked her hand. "No way. She's not a Vestal Virgin."

Everyone argued at once.

Zoe dug her nails into the chair. "I don't have endless time for this. I have clients to subdue."

"Hold that thought." Becca hurried to MJ's desk and pressed the intercom button.

Static crackled.

"Hey." Daemon. His loud chews sounded. When he wasn't necking with Heather or restraining a client, he was eating. "Is that you, Heather? Are you and MJ trying on your leather stuff again? If so, don't forget the chastity thongs. I like those on you." He chuckled. "Better still, I like them off. Whoo."

Heather's face flamed. She lowered it.

Becca rubbed her forehead. "No. It's me. Becca. What are you doing?"

He belched. "Grabbing a snack. Want me to find Heather for you?"

"She's in MJ's office with me on a work assignment. Can you escort and restrain clients for Zoe during the next two hours?"

Constance chimed in, "Better make it three. Just to be sure."

Becca nodded. "Three hours. Once Zoe finishes her special project, she'll relieve you."

"No prob."

Easy for Daemon to say. He didn't have four supernatural beings eyeing him as though he was a lump of clay they were going to mold.

Two hours and forty-three minutes later, Heather held her hands to her chest. Tears brimmed in her eyes.

Constance's turban was askew. Perspiration dampened her matching gown. Becca had pushed her bangs off her forehead an hour ago. Her hair still pointed at the ceiling. MJ lay across her desk, one arm draped over her eyes.

Zoe wanted to bolt, but couldn't, given what she wore. The skirt fit too tightly. This was the nth outfit they'd tried on her and she couldn't even look at it. The other fiascos still danced in her head — everything from porn chic to a Mad Maxine look MJ likened to virginal, at Heather's request. None worked. If anything, they'd made her uglier. "Is this one that bad, too?"

A tear slipped down Heather's cheek.

Zoe's snack threatened to come up. "Oh, hell, it's worse?"

"Hey, hey." Becca pulled Heather into her arms and rubbed her back. "You have to quit falling apart like this."

"I know." She sniffed. "I try, but..." She flapped her hand in Zoe's direction and cried anew.

That was the only answer she needed. Her shoulders and hair pumped smoke worse than an active volcano.

"Whoa." Constance swatted the plumes away. "Knock it off. You'll ruin your look."

MJ groaned. "And after all we did to get you there...here...whatever."

"You mean screw me up even worse than I was?" Zoe gestured wildly. "Look at Heather. She's a basket case because of me."

"She's always like that." Constance shrugged. "She's happy because you're still you, but mega-hot."

Zoe shrank back, not believing it for a minute.

Becca glanced around. "We need a mirror."

"Your wish is my command." MJ moved her forefinger up and down. Popping sounded. Mirrors covered every wall and the ceiling.

Zoe couldn't look.

"Quit being such a baby." Constance grabbed Zoe's arm and hauled her across the room. Presumably to a mirror.

"Go on." Constance shook Zoe. "Open your eyes."

This was harder than learning she'd sold her soul for no good reason, and that had been pissing bad.

"Please look." Heather's voice trembled. "I'm crying because I'm so happy for you."

Wasn't possible. However, good fairies were unable to lie, so this couldn't be that awful. Then again, Heather's fashion sense was monumentally screwed up. Outside of her fetish wear, she rarely donned anything that wasn't pure white.

Steeling herself, Zoe opened one eye and snuck a peak. Her mouth fell open.

"Told ya." Becca pointed to the hall. "Now show those guys how lucky they are to know you. The real you."

Constance took in Zoe's full length and grinned. "This you."

Chapter Eight

Uneven tapping sounded in the hall.

Stefin halted at the odd noise. So did Taro and Anatol.

Tap-tap-tap.

Anatol cupped his ear. "Did you hear that?"

Stefin did but was unable to identify the noise. Could be a para had freed himself from the restraints, hurt a leg in the process and was lurching toward them for revenge. Stefin couldn't wait to tear the fool apart. He glanced over.

A young woman approached on four-inch heels, one uncertain step at a time. Her black stilettos made the tapping noises. Ribbons crisscrossed the tops to tie in bows behind her ankles. Decidedly sexy yet oddly sweet too. Her slim black skirt hugged her hips and legs. The hem fell to mid-calf. A long slit on the right exposed half her thigh.

Stefin doubted she could have walked if not for that opening.

The neckline on her scarlet silk blouse plunged south. Not enough to be indecent, closer to provocative when she turned a certain way. Which she did now to steady herself. The half cups on her bra plumped her small boobs and exposed her rosy nipples. They poked the lustrous fabric. She wore her black hair in a wavy style, parted on the side like Megan Fox sometimes did.

Stefin wasn't certain what to think. This young woman's flawless complexion was too pale to be Megan's, her eyes dark as night and flaming.

He froze.

Zoe? Was it possible? Fuck, yeah, it *was* her.

She looked un-fucking-believable, like a cover girl for *Demon Daily*, Hell's most popular tabloid. He couldn't figure what had happened to her facial piercings and schoolgirl outfit.

Taro and Anatol growled low and long, the sound demons make when they're prepared to ravish.

Stefin put out his arms, blocking both from advancing.

Zoe reached them.

Down the hall, Becca, Constance, Heather and MJ peeked around the corner.

Wary, Stefin waited for the worst.

Becca shoved the others from sight and disappeared with them.

His wish come true. Tonight, he didn't want anyone interrupting his carnal pleasure. Unruly desire made him hotter than usual. He offered a seductive grin and reached for Zoe.

"No." Tottering back, she flapped her hands to keep from falling over.

Stefin couldn't figure out why she'd dodged him. Hell, she was dressed to thrill a demon, him in particular.

"We need to talk." She wobbled and wiggled past him and the others. "In my office." She gestured for them to follow.

Taro and Anatol were on Zoe's heels, sniffing like rutting animals.

Stefin caught up and shoved them aside.

Anatol bounced off the wall then rammed into Stefin.

Taro joined the fray.

Squeezed between them, Stefin's breath whooshed out.

Zoe stopped and looked over.

He and the others stilled.

She regarded each for a long moment. "Are you fighting?"

Her voice sounded nearly as husky as his did.

Too bad he couldn't tell if she was aroused or pissed. Thankfully, he was able to lie easily and shook his head. The others did, too, as well-behaved as saints, for now. Her musky scent was too enchanting for Stefin to argue about anything. Surely, they were going to her office to ball themselves crazy. No way would Becca barge in there since it was Zoe's private space.

They should have thought to use it earlier rather than the break room.

Zoe stopped at the jamb, sagged against it and gestured them inside.

As always, Stefin led. Anatol brought up the rear.

Before Zoe could close and lock the door, Stefin's clothes were history, his naked cock ready for anything.

Taro and Anatol were the same.

She stared at their nudity. Her gaze went blurry. The way a woman should look when facing the demon of her dreams.

Stefin stepped toward her.

Zoe blinked and pointed at the clothes strewn about her office. "Get dressed. This isn't a hotel."

Neither was the break room. She'd had no trouble screwing around there. Maybe she wanted to indulge in roleplaying. Her behaving like a Dominatrix, demanding they do a striptease for her. With any luck, Stefin could convince her that wasn't something he'd ever consider and she wouldn't go bananas on him. "Why do we need to get dressed? Come now, tell me. I promise I won't get mad."

"I can't believe you said that."

"What?"

"That you have the right to be upset when I ask you to do something reasonable here."

She was back to being boss-ma'am. He wasn't crazy enough to challenge her rude comment or tell her there was nothing sensible about this. Not if he wanted to get laid. "Forget what I said."

"I'd already planned to." She teetered to her desk, leaned against it and released her breath. "We need to talk."

"Why?"

She clenched her jaw and crossed her ankles. The skirt fell away from her thigh.

Sexy and bitchy simultaneously. Stefin couldn't imagine what had happened to make her like this. Dressed to entice, yet giving him a hard time. He acquiesced, for now and used his power to dress.

Taro and Anatol did the same.

After everyone was decent again, for the second damn time tonight, Zoe regarded the bulges behind their flies. Color rose to her cheeks. Longing softened her features.

As far as Stefin was concerned, her attitude adjustment was too damn late. She should have thought about what she wanted before she'd ordered them to put on their clothes. "Change your mind?"

"What? No. I'm definitely through with celibacy."

He traded a glance with Anatol and Taro, hoping they'd know if she expected them to undress again since she'd had her little talk and told them the score.

They looked as clueless as he felt.

Zoe crossed her arms. "However…"

Ah yes, the *but*. Women always had a but waiting.

"We all need to compromise." She squared her shoulders. "That's what I'm proposing."

Stefin shook his head. "You'll have to help me out. I haven't a clue what you're talking about."

Taro lifted his shoulders. "Me neither."

Anatol rubbed his chin. "Same here."

Her smile said she enjoyed their confusion. "You guys want me to submit to you, right? To do whatever you want, when you want, correct? I suspect that includes the other parts of BDSM besides submission?"

Stefin nodded vigorously.

Taro and Anatol did, too.

"Okay." She regarded them intently. "Let's say I'm willing to do that."

In that case, Christmas had come early this year. Stefin gave her his most intimate smile. When he'd flashed it at other female demons, they were known to give their allegiance to him rather than offering their loyalty to Satan.

A faint blush crept up Zoe's throat to her face. "However…"

He hated that word. "What?"

"It will only be pretend."

"What's that supposed to mean?"

"I'm still in charge here. You'll do whatever I say, without question, while we're in this place. Once we're out for the night, I'm yours." She leaned toward them. Her neckline fell forward, revealing more of her lacy black bra and nipples. "Make that all yours. I'll pretend to surrender. *Pretend*, got it?" She shrugged. "We'll see what happens."

Taro spoke before Stefin could. "Starting now?"

"After work, not a second before. Do we have a deal?"

What a surprise she'd turned out to be. She could have taught Satan a thing or two about negotiations. "If we don't agree?"

Surprise and dismay crossed her face. She killed her reactions. "We don't have a deal. Simple as that. You'll still do what I say here, since I'm in charge. However, once we leave for the night, I'll do whatever I damn well please."

With another demon, no doubt.

Anatol pulled back his dreadlocks. "I'm on board."

Taro rocked on his heels. "Count me in."

Zoe gave them a shameless smile then regarded Stefin and waited for his answer, her gaze cornering him.

He didn't much like that or her compromise. When she submitted, which she would, he wanted her to do so from free will, because she craved their carnal games as much as he did. More importantly, because she trusted that he, Anatol and Taro would never hurt her. Stefin wasn't as dumb as the others thought. He understood Zoe's ballsy manner masked her heartache and doubt, even now. No way would he ever add to her sorrow.

She should have recognized that. Pissed that she didn't, he answered the only way he could. "Whatever."

"Excellent. Now get back to work so we can take off in an hour."

Taro couldn't get over the change in Zoe or figure out where her confidence had come from. He guessed a potion or spell. Not that the source mattered. He liked what she'd become. Although she'd been a temptress in the break room, her behavior then had been mostly lust and bluff. With her newfound self-assurance, she was a force to be reckoned with, just as Anatol had said when he'd seen her awards.

Taro stopped him and Stefin in the hall. "Where will we take her tonight? Literally." He kept his voice low. "The break room again?"

"Of course not." Anatol flicked fuzz off his sleeve. "It's hardly conducive to a good time. We could use my place."

"No." Stefin pointed at Taro. "Yours, either."

Fine with him. He lived in a studio apartment a gnat would have found confining. The only place he could afford since Becca had warned him not to use his supernatural powers to get something better. During their initial interview, she said he was duty-bound to pay for his digs using what he'd earned here. Wasn't much, given the shitty wages she offered. However, she was the boss and Satan had clued her in on the trouble Taro had caused in Hell for the elites who ran the gambling halls. For that, he was on strict probation. "Where then?"

Surely not the dump Stefin called home. His apartment was as bad as Taro's and Anatol's. They were paying the price for being bad boys in the underworld.

"The perfect place." Stefin offered nothing more.

Zoe couldn't stop shaking. She wasn't certain whether it was due to happiness, shock at what just happened or the pains shooting up her legs from her damn stilettos.

Gritting her teeth, she forced herself to tough it out. The heels were too cute to take off. Dammit, they made her look hot, the same as her outfit and everything else Becca, Constance, MJ and Heather had done to and for her. Especially Heather. She'd healed the holes from the piercings in Zoe's face, leaving her skin perfect so she could wow her guys.

Through eternity and beyond, she would recall Stefin, Taro and Anatol's shock as she'd lurched down the hall, terrified she'd keel over.

They hadn't only eyeballed her in surprise they'd behaved as men do when they're uncertain of themselves. They gave her their power and pussyfooted around, afraid to piss her off or lose her.

Nothing had ever felt as good.

Not that she was smug about it. She figured their deference wouldn't last once their real natures returned. For now, though, she wanted to twirl around her office and dance in delight.

The first painful step made her groan. Tensing at the agony, she staggered to the treatment room and the last client for the day.

After him, watch out.

Eager to get rolling, Anatol kept making mistakes. The fact that he couldn't pay attention to anything except Zoe didn't help.

He loved her amazingly feminine and sexy heels. Her skirt was the best ever. That baby would give him a hard-on after Satan's worst punishments. Her blouse wasn't bad, either. Its delicate fabric showed off her peaked nipples that her bra exposed. And her face…

Who would've believed she was so pretty, not cute as he'd first thought.

He lost his grasp on the were who was limp from treatment. The guy's ass hit the floor, followed by his shoulders and head.

Stefin snarled. "Hurt him anymore than that and we'll be stuck here until dawn."

Taro's glare said he agreed. "Hey, you." He shook the were's shoulder. "Anything broken?"

"Uh…" He pushed to his elbows and sagged back down. "Just bruised, I think."

"Great. That'll save you some bucks on healing. I'll call Heather in here."

"That's okay. I'm pinching pennies for this condo I have my eye on. The babes are gonna love it. I'll heal on my own."

"Sounds like a plan. I'll help you out." Taro flung him over his shoulder and spoke to everyone. "I'll put him outside then lock the front door. Be right back."

Zoe twisted the middle button on her blouse. It broke away from the fabric and made the V on her neckline even deeper, fully revealing her black bra.

Anatol's cock stiffened and tried to point at her.

Footfalls pounded in the hall. Panting, Taro returned to the room. "He's outside, crawling down the stairs. We're finished. Let's go."

"Yes, let's." Stefin lifted his hand.

"Wait." Zoe grabbed his arm. "No powers."

She couldn't be serious. "*Chérie.*" Anatol cradled her cheek. A feather couldn't be softer. If she wasn't beneath him soon, he'd go mad. "We used our powers in the break room. Was that so horrible?"

Her lids slid down then snapped back up. "It was when Becca showed up."

"That was only because Stefin stupidly forgot to secure the door. Don't make the rest of us suffer because he's a moron."

Stefin growled.

"No fighting. And he's not that. Not even close." She rested her hands on their chests and shivered. "You know how I feel about using our powers."

Taro cupped her chin. "If we don't tonight, you'll have to walk to where we're going. It's several miles."

Her complexion paled substantially. "We could take my hearse. I gassed it up this morning."

"Driving will take time." Anatol brushed his lips over her cheek. "Do you really want to delay this?" He licked her earlobe.

She leaned against him. "I suppose it would be all right this one—"

Crackling air drowned her out. It built to a stiff breeze then died down. One minute, they'd been in the office. Now they stood next to an empty table in the Crucible. Its atmosphere smoky, dark and noisy as fuck from the heavy metal band that played.

This couldn't be Stefin's perfect place.

Zoe craned her neck and gaped.

At the next table, a nude couple screwed frantically, as if the hounds of Hell might stop them before they climaxed.

Stefin bumped her shoulder. "About what you said in the office…"

"Huh? What?"

He repeated his comment.

She blinked slowly and dragged her attention to him. "Said?"

"Yeah. After you came down the hall wearing that." He gestured to her outfit. "And told us to hop to and pile in your office, which we did."

"Uh-huh."

The couple bellowed and gave each other a high-five. Zoe watched.

Stefin eased her face back. "Pay attention."

"I have been." Her gaze zipped everywhere.

"I meant, to me. Back at the office, you said we should do exactly what you demanded at work. We did. Now it's your turn to give us what we want."

Wasn't the smoothest line Anatol had ever heard, but he had to admit, it laid out the ground plan.

Zoe swayed a bit but didn't renege.

"Hey, guys, welcome back." The waitress they'd had the other night snuck up through the heavy smoke. She bobbed her head in greeting to Zoe. "What's your pleasure?"

Anatol touched Zoe's hand. "Are you hungry?"

She nodded.

Stefin pressed closer. "For what exactly?"

Her cheeks and throat colored. She swung her finger from him to Anatol then to Taro.

The waitress grinned widely, showing her fangs. "I'll be back later."

Taro slipped his arm around Zoe's waist. "Bend over the table, legs spread, ass high."

Zoe didn't budge. She had expected they'd take her somewhere secluded tonight and her clothes would whizz off as they had in the break room. Which seemed a thousand lifetimes ago.

Nothing happened here except for her rough breathing and lightheadedness that hit hard, making her wobble. She gripped the table to keep from falling.

The banshee band shrieked the lyrics to their song, their ghostly bods clad in black leather and lace.

Zoe sweated worse than they did.

Stefin pressed his mouth to her ear. "What are you waiting for?"

His lips were outrageously soft, his breath a caress.

Time to get with the program and whatever they wanted. That was the deal.

She hadn't considered it would include voyeurism. Not that the male patrons would gawk for long. They were busy ravaging their own babes. The ones across the room were in positions she hadn't believed possible. The guy's legs were wrapped around his date's head *and* her torso, like they'd spiraled around them several times. She appeared to have more than two arms. Possibly four. Unless the second pair were her thighs and calves.

"Zoe?"

She looked at Stefin. He faded in and out with the bass from the music. A monster's heartbeat couldn't have been louder. "Yeah?"

"What are you waiting for?"

Courage to do this, considering her bod. The makeover hadn't given her a C cup or hips. "Nothing." Trembling badly, she rested her forearms on the table, lifted her ass and spread her legs as well as she could. Her tight skirt wasn't cooperating.

Stefin settled behind her. He eased the garment past her thighs and folded it on her waist to reveal her ass.

She sucked air. Unlike the chaste white panties she usually wore, tonight she sported a skimpy thong. MJ's idea. She'd promised the guys would love it.

Zoe certainly did despite her previous misgivings about this place. She felt deliciously exposed, wonderfully used.

Stefin squeezed her bare cheeks, his enthusiasm unbridled. He touched her anus the same way.

She held her breath.

Anatol climbed on the table and crawled toward her like an animal in the wild. The flames in his eyes were so bright they nearly blinded her. He sat on his heels, spread his legs widely and unzipped his fly.

Perspiration ran down Zoe's temple to her cheek. The band screeched even louder, their thunderous music thumping in her belly. With Stefin and Anatol in place, Taro reclined on the table to her right and slipped his hand inside her blouse then beneath her bra cups. Watching her closely, he cupped her boobs and brushed her nipples.

Delight barreled through her. She lost what little breath she'd had.

Anatol released his cock from his boxer briefs and fly the mortal way then lifted his crown to her mouth.

Eagerly, she accepted his offering. He tasted as wicked as she recalled, all man and demon, demanding his due. Giving it, she eased his full length inside.

He growled happily.

Taro pinched and plucked her nipples exactly as she liked. Stefin pulled her thong down.

Heated air brushed her delicate folds, reminding Zoe how vulnerable and wet she was.

Stefin stroked her opening.

She trembled at his intimate touch and the corrupt atmosphere that made her crave more. To wait a second longer for satisfaction would be cruel. She needed him, Taro and Anatol to take her now.

Stefin entered her fully in one hard, assured thrust.

Zoe stilled.

Anatol pressed closer, wanting her attention.

She licked him wantonly but couldn't dismiss Stefin. They fit so well and closely, Zoe wasn't certain where she ended and he began. Never had she been as filled, not even by a demon she once hooked up with whose size was legendary. Stefin beat him and the others in Hell. His enormous rod stretched her pussy and made certain she gave it a home.

She couldn't do anything less. As she squeezed her inner muscles around his shaft, she pleasured Anatol's cock and lifted her torso to give Taro better access to her breasts.

Several demons strode over. Their rich sulfur-and-musk scents betrayed their lust. They smiled hungrily.

Stefin thrust, his strokes powerful, his balls tapping her.

Zoe's vision dimmed.

He rubbed her clit.

Too much delight tore through her, making her feel wonderfully depraved. She gripped the table to control herself.

Stefin let loose and pumped faster. He rubbed her clit harder. Anatol eased his cock from her mouth and drove it back inside, making certain she took in every inch. Taro sagged to the table, pulled her bra and blouse aside then latched on to her breast, driving her closer to nirvana.

Zoe fought for control, not to mention a decent breath. She couldn't manage either. Competing feelings warred within her from what each guy did.

She broke and gasped her release around Anatol's cock. He came next, followed by Stefin, both spilling their demon seed into her. The sounds they made were obscene but beautiful and mingled with the savage music.

Anatol slumped back. His shaft slipped from her mouth.

Taro rolled off the table for his turn in her pussy. He pushed Stefin aside. Another demon materialized from nowhere and gripped her hips. Taro shoved him away.

The demon's arms windmilled. He righted himself. "You are so going to regret that."

"Bullcrap. You want a piece of me, come and take it. I don't reckon you're man or demon enough to do anything, except whine like a damn female."

Patrons paused in their raunchy activities. Several ladies sucked in a breath at Taro's insult.

A huge dude appeared through the heavy smoke. He wore a black tee that had the word *Bouncer* emblazoned across his chest. "Fight if you want. But no fucking powers. Settle this like mortals. Anything breaks, you pay for it. Cold. Hard. Cash. We don't accept checks and magic is off-limits here."

Taro growled. "Fine with me."

Fists and curses flew. Juvenile to the extreme, but Zoe loved having him and the other guy battle over her.

Taro landed an epic punch. The demon crashed onto a table, destroying it, and rolled across the floor then lay still. Taro's shoulders heaved with his rough breaths. Auburn locks hung over his forehead.

She grinned.

He plowed his rod into her channel.

No supernatural power could match his virility and strength. He freaking owned her. She cried her thanks.

Stefin settled on the table, pants still undone, his cock and balls exposed. Her scent perfumed both. His rod filled her mouth.

Anatol played with her boobs.

A muscular demon planted his hands on his narrow hips. "Me and my buddies are next."

"In your dreams." Stefin growled loud enough to shatter several drinking glasses and bottles. "Zoe belongs to us."

Tears pricked her eyes at his desire for her. What she liked to believe was his protectiveness. Didn't matter if it lasted or not. She had now and opened herself to him, Anatol and Taro, ready to risk anything, including future heartache.

These moments were worth it.

The other demons hurled oaths but drifted away.

Taro rode her without pause, as if no one else existed except her and him.

He was an exquisite lover, more tender than Stefin but impassioned nonetheless. His thrusts showed stunning expertise. So did his fervent strokes on her clit. She alternately tensed from desire and went limp, submitting fully.

Stefin used her mouth as he had her pussy, his mastery and pure abandon a marvel. Anatol sucked her nipple that Taro hadn't gotten to.

She soared, peaked and had an out-of-body experience. Looking down on herself, Zoe couldn't have been more pleased. She actually rocked her outfit. The guys looked good no matter what they did or didn't wear.

Taro and Stefin climaxed. Their rapturous cries competed with the other racket and brought her back to Earth.

Wearing a blissful smile, Stefin keeled over, spent for the moment.

Taro kissed her back.

She wiggled her ass into his groin.

"My turn." Anatol shouldered Taro aside.

Before Taro could climb onto the table as the others had and slip his rod into her mouth, Anatol dipped his fingers in her cunt then brushed the moisture on her anus.

To prepare her for his cock.

Chapter Nine

Anatol drew in a ragged breath and ordered himself to slow down, to take care. He didn't want to harm Zoe.

This was about pleasure.

Unfortunately, his balls and rod agreed too eagerly, neither wanted to wait a second longer for relief. He fought his overwhelming lust. His shoulders and neck burned.

If she'd been any other female demon, he would have readily indulged in his beastly urges. Because she was Zoe, he couldn't, even though she was into this.

She lifted her ass, wiggled it, too, inviting him to fill and take her.

Nice, but not enough. During Taro's turn, she'd worn a blissful look like none Anatol had ever seen on a woman's face, mortal or supernatural. Taro had taken her gently at first and slowly built to a crescendo that had culminated in spectacular desire.

If a dumb cowboy could do that, a demon with Anatol's skill could send her over the moon. If he could only calm down long enough to control himself. His cock grew harder and thicker, every inch acutely sensitive from unfulfilled need. He wanted to shriek. Clenching his jaw, he ran his crown over Zoe's anus, showing her as much tenderness as he could.

She shuddered.

He froze. "Does it hurt?"

She turned her head to the side. "You haven't done anything yet."

Not true. He kept playing the Bieb's tune *Baby* in his mind, hoping it would deflate his hard-on a little. Any relief was welcomed, so he wouldn't go at Zoe like an animal. "Tell me if it does."

"I will. But it won't."

Taro eased her face to his. He stroked her cheek and guided his thick rod into her mouth. Zoe sighed contentedly, her focus on him alone.

Anatol seethed. Taro already had his pleasure with her and had no right to horn in on anyone else's.

Determined to show her the best time ever, Anatol stroked her clit, his touch light but precise.

She moaned contentedly around Taro's intrusive cock.

Encouraged, Anatol probed her tightest opening with his crown and slid it inside carefully. Her snugness squeezed him. Her heat made him yearn for more. He gathered what little breath he could and stilled to gauge her response.

Zoe arched her back, which lifted her ass. An eager welcome to a randy demon if ever there was one.

Savage craving rolled through him. Too far gone to resist, he worked his full crown inside her passage and went dizzy as fuck. Her close fit and warmth had no equal. He stroked her back, delighted at his black skin against her pale flesh.

Despite the noise in here and Taro's rod in her mouth, her pleading whimper broke through, signaling her desire for more.

Anatol penetrated, his rod deep within her. At any other time, their joining would have satisfied. Tonight, he required a different closeness and laced his fingers with hers.

She squeezed hard and held tight.

Forgotten emotions rushed through him. He pressed his cheek to her shoulder.

She flexed her passage around his shaft, proving she liked how near he was.

He had no objection to this profane yet surprisingly sacred act.

They held onto each other like star-crossed lovers from a sentimental romance rather than the doomed who demanded and expected mindless pleasure. He pumped easily to test her endurance.

Accepting his invasion, she softened beneath him. Her throaty purr convinced him he'd pleased her.

Unable to contain his joy, Anatol forgot his manners and growled worse than Stefin ever had.

Stefin jerked and awakened. "You're still not through?" He ran his hand down his face. "Hurry up."

Nothing in Hell or Heaven could make Anatol rush this. He blew a tress away from Zoe's neck and kissed her there. She tightened her inner muscles around his cock.

The damn thing practically leaped in delight. He sucked hard, giving her a hickey to memorialize this moment, then got down to business. He knew he couldn't take much more delay. Straightening, he gripped her hips so she couldn't escape. Not that he figured she'd try, given how she pushed into him.

For that, he'd always be grateful.

At a measured pace, he thrust, the friction between them so great his hair practically stood on end. Puffing hard, he pumped faster and stroked her clit, alternating his touch between gentle and rough.

Perspiration shone on her shoulders. She couldn't keep still and pushed her ass into him, embracing each thrust.

He gave her his all. Nothing less would do.

She came on a startled gasp and howled around Taro's cock still in her mouth.

Anatol's control weakened. He shuddered and fought for restraint, needing to outdo Taro and Stefin, at least in Zoe's mind. He rode her for ages and reluctantly surrendered to his orgasm, his chin lifted to the ceiling. If he could have managed a breath, he would have roared his relief.

Patrons' rowdy shouts and the wailing band punched up the noise level several decibels.

The room dipped and swayed. Conversations drifted close then faded before he could catch the words, everything surreal and magical. Nothing could compare to being deep inside a woman he desired.

As his climax drained away, he lowered himself to Zoe and held her as close as he could.

After Stefin and Taro enjoyed her again, they and Anatol decided the next course would be food rather than her.

Zoe slumped, too bummed to keep up her Ms. Independent act.

Stefin touched her nose with his. "What's wrong?"

"You guys. I thought you had bigger appetites."

Anatol and Taro laughed.

Stefin licked the healing wounds the vamp had left on her. "You're dessert."

Sweeter words didn't exist. Ravenous, she couldn't decide what to choose as far as food went. The extensive menu covered everything on Earth and in Hell, each dish tempting beyond belief. Odd for her. Since being damned, she'd lost her appetite and had to force stuff down her throat. Except for chocolate.

Right now, she wanted anything edible.

Tonight had been better than she'd dreamed possible, and almost exactly what she required. The guys craving, using and pleasuring her. Gifting her with orgasm after orgasm. Decorating her with more hickeys than Angelina Jolie had tats.

Almost paradise. If only they loved her...

She needed that badly, but wasn't about to hope for a miracle. Better to go with the flow. Once she and the guys had fixed their clothes, Stefin pulled her onto his lap and settled his arm around her waist, his cock against her ass.

Taro scowled.

"What's this?" Anatol's gesture took in her and Stefin. "You intend to hog Zoe for yourself? You're back to thinking you run things?"

"Not think, know." Stefin shrugged. "As it should be." He pressed his face to her neck. "Still can't decide what you'd like for supper?"

His breath was heated and sweet, making her toes curl, the same as Taro and Anatol wanting her.

She ruffled Stefin's hair. "It all looks good. Sorry."

"No need to be." He handed the menu to the waitress. "Bring everything."

She fanned herself with the laminated pages. "You got the dough for that? Last time you three were here, you only gave me a one-percent tip. Give me two tonight, and I may be able to afford that yacht I've had my eye on."

The guys' faces colored.

They were proud demons, used to having whatever their powers could grant them. It hadn't been easy for them to do things the mortal way and to settle for the slave wages Becca offered. She wasn't an unfair boss. Satan had requested the shitty pay to teach the guys a lesson in humility.

Zoe would have offered to settle the check herself but didn't want to humiliate them further. However, there was another solution. "You're off the clock. During that time, supernatural powers rule."

Stefin grinned. Taro and Anatol weren't as enthused.

Anatol tapped his fork against the table. "You heard the bouncer. This place is cash only."

"You could conjure some up, couldn't you?" She spoke to the waitress, "Would that be okay or is it breaking the rules?"

"Give me a twenty percent tip and my lips are sealed."

"That's doable, right, guys?" Before they could respond or argue, she wanted to reassure them. "Tonight, you can be bad boys. I won't tell."

Taro spoke to the waitress. "Everything then. We're starving."

As the guys waited for the meal, they took turns fondling and kissing Zoe. She staggered from lap to lap, undone by passion. When the food arrived, she was snuggled against Anatol, twisting his dreadlocks around her fingers.

The waitress set up the feast. For Stefin, there was *blini*, *vareniky*, salmon and potato salad, borscht with meat, *piroshki*, powdered-sugar teacakes, orange drop cookies and a liter of vodka. Anatol had Camembert, *crêpes*, *blanquette de veau*, *soupe à l'oignon*, *hachis parmentier*, various pastries and wine. Taro's fare was less sophisticated — fried chicken, rabbit stew, black bean chili, buffalo steak, apple pie à la mode and a bottle of whiskey.

Never having cared for the bland food during the Puritan era, Zoe sampled the guys' dishes. Her taste buds came alive. She gobbled everything as fast as she could.

"*Chérie.*" Anatol eased her hand from the fare. "Slow down."

"Why? I'm hungry."

"And you'll get your fill, I swear." He held a *crêpe* between his teeth and encouraged her to nibble the other end.

Did she ever, not stopping until their lips touched. They necked and sucked each other's tongue until they both needed air.

She repeated the process with Stefin and Taro. They held beef and buffalo meat between their lips. When she finished swallowing, they each licked sauce or juices from her mouth, kissed her savagely then started over, offering new taste sensations, letting her sample everything.

Giving her the best night ever.

Thoroughly stuffed and unwilling to consider the future, Zoe surrendered to hedonism as she hadn't before. She boogied with her guys to deafening music that would have broken a mortal's eardrums, threw back vodka shots with Stefin, sipped Anatol's wine and licked whiskey from Taro's lips.

Good times, even if they'd be fleeting.

* * * *

Zoe woke in her own bed, hungover and alone. How she'd gotten to her apartment or why the guys hadn't joined her wasn't something she could answer. She sat up, dropped back down and gripped the mattress. The room spun too wildly for her to be vertical. After several deep breaths, she crawled from room to room searching for a note from them. There wasn't any. They hadn't sent texts or left voicemails, either.

She shouldn't have been surprised. The enchanting date was over, another cruddy evening here, good times at an end.

Crestfallen, she dragged to the office before anyone else got there, her temples pounding, stomach roiling, feet throbbing.

She rested her head on her desk. The room lurched worse that way but she didn't have the strength to sit upright. At any other time, she would have hurled and taken a sick day. Wasn't possible now. She had to talk to her guys and find out what had happened last night after she'd blacked out.

Zoe hoped she hadn't bitched at them or worse, confessed her love. That would be the absolute pits.

The last she recalled, they'd carried her on their shoulders during a Russian folk dance. She vaguely remembered the crowd cheering and Anatol losing his grip on her, followed by Taro then Stefin.

Her sore hip proved they'd dropped her. What had happened after that was a mystery. Could be they'd found someone new to shake a leg with.

Her stomach churned. No male demon could have resisted the waitress's attractive fangs. Even though the band members were hideous, as banshees generally were, they did have big boobs and curvy hips.

She hit her desk, hating her doubt, jealousy and stupid figure. Pre-teens were built better than she was. She should have let MJ fix that during the makeover.

"Zoe?"

Heather. Zoe folded her arms over her head.

Unfortunately, her misery played to Heather's sympathetic nature. "Are you all right? You seem kind of — oh, my God." She inhaled sharply. "What did you do to your feet?"

They were twice their normal size, her skin oozing over the ribbons. Last night Zoe's feet had turned maroon. She hadn't had the nerve to look at them before she came here, nor had she wanted to ditch the stilettos. They were so hot.

Heather fell to her knees. "Let me heal you."

"Don't hurt the heels."

"I may have to cut them off first to get to your feet."

"*No.*" Zoe sat up so fast the room whirled wildly. She hung on to her desk and breathed hard. "I just need to get used to them and the rest of my clothes."

She'd lost all but one button on her blouse last night, how she couldn't recall. The slit in her skirt was even higher, showing her thong. Only her bra was unscathed and thankfully so. It gave her contours nature hadn't.

Heather sat on her heels. "You're not going to ever change from those clothes?"

She hadn't planned to. "They're sexy. I don't have anything else that comes close to this. I'm not going back to my schoolgirl outfit, all right?"

"Of course not. The blouse and plaid skirt didn't do you justice. Not that I thought they were boring or anything. I didn't. It's just that — "

"I get it. Thanks. No need to apologize."

"Okay. Sorry." She rubbed Zoe's shoulder. "Would you like MJ to come up with something else for you to wear tonight?"

It was already evening, the only time vamps could come in for their treatments. "You mean now?"

"No. Although I'm sure MJ would be happy to do that, too. I meant after work."

"What's after work?"

"I don't know. Didn't Stefin, Taro and Anatol tell you?"

Zoe blinked repeatedly, trying to get Heather into focus. Currently, there was two of her swimming to the right, the left… "About what?"

"Stefin left a voicemail saying he and the others would be a few minutes late for their shifts. They had to make plans for tonight, their evening with you."

That wasn't possible. Zoe figured she'd passed out and was dreaming or hallucinating this. "What?"

Heather repeated what she'd said.

"No, no, no." Zoe tongued her mouth. It tasted shitty. "Are you sure they didn't say they'd be late because they were with another babe? That is, a real babe?"

"Of course, I'm certain. Why would they say that?"

It was the only thing that seemed logical. Zoe had never been any man's first choice. When it came to three demons who were total hunks, it was unlikely they'd want her over anyone else. They may have had fun last night, but she'd ended up in bed alone. Clear proof what they thought of her.

She guessed.

Totally confused, she gripped Heather's shoulder. "I need advice."

"Sure. Do you want me to get Becca?"

"No." She pushed Heather back to her knees. "Do guys usually return to their own places after having a good time with a woman? Did Daemon do that with you?"

Heather's face flushed to the same shade Zoe's feet had been last night. "Ah, he would've had to walk back to Couturie. That's a long way from my apartment. Remember how worried I was about that when he was here and how Becca asked if you would drive him?" Her mouth turned down. "You said only if you could hogtie and lash him to the roof."

Zoe didn't recall that. "So, he never left your place?"

"He couldn't."

"Why?"

"He didn't look like a satyr anymore after his treatment. It's not like he could have returned to where he used to live. No one would have recognized him without a tail, horns or hooves. Remember me telling you, Constance and Becca that? I didn't want to risk the other satyrs ganging up on him and doing who knows what. I doubt he would have minded. He's really brave. Sometimes I think…"

Zoe stopped listening and tried to compare Heather's romance with her own. It was like mixing apples and kumquats. Daemon had fallen for Heather fast and fully, the real reason he never left her place. Stefin, Taro and Anatol were only interested in a good time. For the moment, that appeared to be with her, if they were going to take her out tonight.

She massaged her temples.

Becca, Constance and MJ poured into her office. After checking out Zoe's ruined clothes, Constance gave her two thumbs-up. MJ made an O with her thumb and forefinger, indicating success.

Becca sniffed. "You smell like a distillery."

"Better than sulfur." Constance regarded everyone. "Amirite?"

Becca threw her a warning glance, focused on Zoe and gaped at her feet. "Good God, can't you take those heels off?"

"I don't want to." She pulled her feet under the chair despite how much it hurt to move them. "They're fine. They don't ache nearly as bad as my head does."

Constance wiggled her eyebrows. "Fun night, huh?"

Zoe grinned. Pain shot across her skull. She winced.

Becca muttered an oath. "Heather, heal Zoe's hangover and see to her feet."

"No." Zoe leaned away. "I don't have time for that. I need a new outfit for after work tonight."

"You need one for work, too." Becca gestured to Zoe's buttonless blouse and torn skirt. "MJ, can you see to it?"

"Easy-peasy. Just tell me what you want."

Zoe shrugged. "Stefin, Anatol and Taro."

MJ glanced at the others then offered a confused smile. "You're wishing for their hearts? Metaphorically, of course. You want me to—"

"Hold it." Becca sank to her knees and took Zoe's hands. "What happened last night?"

Almost everything Zoe had ever needed except the most important thing—commitment. "Nothing bad. We all had a great time. Some of it I don't even remember."

Constance pumped her fist.

Worry flooded Becca's face, a sure sign a lecture was coming.

Just what she didn't need.

Becca squeezed Zoe's fingers. "You don't think tonight will be as good?"

"Are you kidding? Knowing the guys, it'll probably be even better." Her strained smile faded. "Until they get tired of me and find a real babe to hang out with."

"That again?" Constance clucked her tongue. "Girl, what is wrong with you?"

"For starters, I'm flat-chested." She pulled her hands from Becca. "If you have the rest of the week, I can detail what else isn't right about me."

MJ stroked her throat. "I can give you boobs. All you have to do is wish for them."

"Don't do it." Heather grabbed Zoe's arm. "They're murder to carry around. My back hurt something awful when Becca's potion made mine huge."

All eyes shot to Becca.

She squeezed her fists. "There was nothing wrong with that damn potion. Mom swore by it. Heather went from an A cup to a C just like she wanted. That wasn't failure. It was a success."

"Except Daemon didn't care for them." MJ patted Heather's head. "He likes her the way she is. I can't blame him. Now why she's interested in him is a total mystery to me."

"Stop it." Heather gave MJ a scolding look. "Daemon's perfect."

"If you say so, Precious."

Zoe made a face. "Can we get back to me? Daemon likes Heather as she is because she's already gorgeous and he's in love. I'm working at a disadvantage here."

Becca cradled Zoe's cheek. "Remember when I thought Eric couldn't possibly love someone curvy like me?"

"I do and it was awful. You were hell to work with. Barking orders. Bursting into tears for no damn good reason. Dragging around here like a zombie. Actually, you were worse than a — "

"I get it, all right?" She crossed her arms. "That's not what I meant. Although he did love me, I was too afraid and uncertain to recognize it."

Constance nodded. "You almost screwed that up, big time."

"Listen to them, please." Heather pressed Zoe's hand to her chest. "Give your guys a chance."

She hadn't planned to do anything else. However, the question remained, would Stefin, Anatol and Taro do the same for her? She wasn't sure if they'd invite her into their lives permanently, or if she was doomed to be their plaything for only a little while.

Right now, it was all Zoe had. She could not lose it. "What do you guys suggest I wear here then later?"

"Different shoes for sure." MJ made a face at Zoe's swollen ankles. "Probably something orthopedic."

"What?" Zoe pulled her feet in even more. Agonizing pain ripped up her calves. She groaned.

"Just kidding." MJ winked. "You want hot again?"

"For later, not here." Becca stood. "At the office, she should be elegant. Give the guys a taste of what's to come. Make them want more."

"What if they don't?" Zoe's pain turned to panic. "I don't want them to lose interest."

"They won't." Becca offered a knowing look. "Trust me."

Zoe recalled the fuck-ups from Becca's magic and her strained relationship with Eric before things miraculously turned around. Slumped against her chair, she pinched her nose. "Heather?"

"Yeah?"

"Help me, please."

Using her healing touch, Heather banished Zoe's headache and wooziness in less than a second. Her feet took longer, but at last looked normal again.

Becca insisted Zoe try on several heels this time and walk in them before deciding on which to wear. "You want a good fit. Something that supports your arches."

Heather scrolled through the Net on her smartphone. "Maybe she should use some of these Dr. Scholl's things."

Zoe curled her upper lip. "Those are for elderly people. I'm not even three-hundred-and-fifty years old yet."

"A regular baby." MJ fluffed her hair. "I've got thousands of years on you and I wouldn't use them, either."

Zoe spoke to Heather, "See?"

She pulled in her shoulders. "Sorry."

"No reason to be." Constance hugged Heather. "You were only trying to help." She leveled her gaze on Zoe. "We all are."

That they were. More clothes filled Zoe's office than the local Macy's. Not knowing what to choose, she gestured helplessly. "I can't make up my mind. Everything's beginning to look the same to me."

"Leave it to us." Becca rifled through a rack with blouses and pants in every color known to woman. "We didn't let you down last time."

They hadn't, but Zoe couldn't relax. The other staffers were arriving. Clients, too. Howls, shrieks and wails filled the place.

Ordinarily, that would have been music to her ears. Since she'd met Stefin, Anatol and Taro, she needed to hear their rough voices and them slamming into walls during their fights.

She worried she'd never experience those precious sounds again because they wouldn't show up. Ever. Could be Stefin had lied in his voicemail. He was a demon after all. He and the others might have returned to the Crucible, preferring it because they'd met a female demon last night who truly revved their engines.

Zoe chewed her lip. MJ's selections appeared on her then disappeared the moment Becca, Constance or Heather shook their heads, which they did continually.

At last, Becca held up her hand. "Stop. That's it."

Constance nodded. Heather clapped.

"Now for your hair." MJ spoke to the others, "Still elegant?"

Becca smiled. "Exactly. No, wait, sophisticated, too."

Zoe waved her hands to get their attention. "I think the guys like hot."

Constance sniffed. "Guys like what you teach them to like."

Maybe for her but she'd never been with the unholy trio.

Too weary to debate the point, Zoe closed her eyes, surrendered to their decisions and awaited the outcome.

Someone bumped her shoulder. Given the seductive fragrance, it had to be MJ. "Go on. Look."

Even before Zoe could gather the courage, she figured she had a lot on. Fabric covered her arms, thighs and calves. Surely, they hadn't dressed her in a burka. Not even the horniest demon would drool over that.

Feeling sick, she opened her eyes and stared at her reflection in the cheval mirror MJ had set up. They'd dressed her in a silky blouse and pants that had stovepipe legs, both garments in midnight blue. The color enhanced Zoe's complexion, making it seem less sallow, more delicate. The heels on her black pumps were only three inches high, the toe section cut out. They'd swept up her hair in a French roll. Tendrils grazed her temples and cheeks.

Elegant and sophisticated, just as Becca had envisioned. Yet oddly sexy, too.

Zoe smiled.

"We're here," Stefin's voice boomed down the hall.

She grinned like a lovesick teen then gestured frantically. "Get rid of this stuff before they see it. I want them to think I look this way all the time."

Constance frowned. "Since yesterday?"

"Quiet." Becca elbowed MJ. "Lose this stuff."

"Your wish is my—"

"Zoe?" Stefin's footfalls neared the door.

She bounced on her heels. Popping sounds filled the room. The clothes and mirror disappeared.

"Hold it." MJ grabbed Zoe's arm and pulled her back. "What kind of outfit do you need for tonight?"

"I don't know."

"Wait here." Constance hurried past them into the hall. "Hey, guys." She waved. "Good to see you. Stay where you are. I need a word."

Constance's high-pitched murmurs flowed into Zoe's office, joined by the guys' voices. Those sounds were so deep her pussy ached for what she'd experienced last night. However, they spoke too softly, keeping her from catching their words.

Everything quieted. Footfalls approached.

Zoe backed away from the door, so did Becca, Heather and MJ.

Constance hurried inside and beamed at Zoe. "You lucky girl."

"Why? What happened?"

"I know where they're taking you tonight." She wagged her finger.

Zoe wasn't following. She leaned against the desk for support. "Where are they taking me?"

"You'll see...in time. Don't worry, we'll make sure you're well-prepared." She pressed her mouth to MJ's ear and whispered furiously.

For the first time ever, MJ blushed. "You're right. Lucky girl."

Chapter Ten

Stefin huddled with Taro and Anatol to discuss the evening's plans.

Zoe shot into the hall, regained her balance and glared over her shoulder at something or someone in her office.

Probably whoever had pushed her.

It didn't seem possible but she looked even more awesome than she had last night. Her outfit was pure business but sexy, like a toned-down Dominatrix.

Stefin shoved Anatol and Taro away.

They swore.

Smoothing her clothes, Zoe tried to appear casual.

The blazing flames in her eyes contradicted her nonchalance. Perhaps she was recalling last night's events, especially his part in them. He'd had her first, indulging his reckless lust and yearning desire. Once they were through with this shift, they'd play again. Dangerously so.

Zoe wiggled toward them, her balance and grace far better than when she'd worn her other heels. Those shoes had caused a commotion at the Crucible. The ladies coveted them. The guys had envied him, Anatol and Taro all because they were with her.

Even if the others hadn't responded that way, Stefin wouldn't have cared. Partying with Zoe had been a revelation. Not only had he hungered for everything she was, he enjoyed her company. That had never happened with another woman. Zoe was pure fun, up for anything, almost one of the boys, but all woman, too. A real tigress when it came to sex. She'd sucked his cock so much and he'd loved her so well with it the damn thing was just about raw.

Existence didn't get better than this.

"Looks like your feet are doing better today." Her shoes were adorable. The cutouts in the toes stirred his lust and cock. He edged closer. "How's the rest of you faring?"

She blushed prettily. However, her wistful smile turned into an oddly shamed grimace.

He couldn't imagine why. They were demons, already damned. There wasn't any reason to play coy. She sure as hell hadn't at the club. Not only had she gone along with the program, she'd suggested acts that had stoked his, Anatol and Taro's libidos even when they had been past fatigue.

Zoe looked at them expectantly. "What happened last night?"

Stefin exchanged a glance with Taro and Anatol. They looked as confused as he was. He hoped this wasn't a trick question like those she'd pulled on them during their training. "Why?"

"What?"

"Huh?"

She frowned. "Are you stalling?"

He had to get a new act. "What was the question?"

"You are trying not to answer." Her face turned deathly white, like a vamp's or a reaper's. "Why?"

"Let me ask you something first. You don't recall anything?"

She blushed as red as her feet had once been. "Most of it. I think." She mumbled something beneath her breath. "What happened after the folk dance when you guys dropped me? Past that, everything's a blank."

She'd forgotten the best parts.

Anatol gestured the guys to huddle again. "Should we tell her?"

Stefin didn't see the harm since it wasn't anything that could put them in the dog house. "Go on."

"You rode Taro as if he were a horse." Anatol chuckled. "You smacked his ass with a wooden spoon you snatched from the cook after chasing then tripping him in the kitchen. He wanted his utensil back. You refused and kept shouting, 'Ride 'em cowboy'."

Her complexion went gray. "Were we dressed?"

Taro grinned broadly. "Nope. After I bucked and threw you, Anatol, Stefin and two other demons held your arms and legs while I went down on your pussy. Damn, it was sweet."

Zoe clutched her throat and stepped back.

Stefin followed. "You'd barely recovered from that orgasm when you demanded I do sixty-nine with you. How could I refuse?"

Anatol leaned toward her. "Even after Stefin had come three times — bam, bam, bam — you refused to let go of his cock."

Taro snickered. "You kept hollering that you wanted to take it home with you. Ours too."

Stefin would never forget her zeal for his. She'd been lukewarm about the others. "Taro, Anatol and three other demons had to pry you away from my rod. Despite that, you kept fighting them to get to me." He gave her an indulgent smile. "I understand your overwhelming desire, but even I need to rest for a bit after so much activity."

A low moan poured from her throat.

Sounded like she was embarrassed rather than turned on. He couldn't figure out why. Sure, she'd been a siren last night, but in the best possible way.

She cringed. "That's it?"

"You were on me next." Anatol pushed his dreadlocks over his shoulder. "You kept shouting for someone to give you a rope so you could tie me up. When no one brought you any, you tried to use my hair to bind my hands."

Stefin cut in, "When that didn't work, you used your power."

She recoiled, horror edged on her face. "What did I do?"

"Not much." He scratched his neck. "You kept us pinned against the wall while you took our cocks in your mouth and sucked our balls. By the way, that rocks." The glorious pleasure that had roared through him wasn't something he'd ever forget. "We could have freed ourselves but didn't want to upset you."

She dug her fingers into her neck, like she wanted to strangle herself. "Did I say anything during all of this?"

"You kept shouting obscenities." Stefin shrugged. "That alone told me you were having a good time."

"Nothing other than that?"

Taro frowned. "Like what?"

"Never mind." Repeatedly, she stepped back.

They followed.

Soon, everyone turned in circles, her retreating, them pursuing.

Zoe stopped first, her hand on the wall, head down. "How'd I get home? Who put me to bed?"

Anatol gestured to himself, Taro and Stefin.

Another delightful memory. "It took the three of us to hold you down until you passed out."

She groaned. "And you left. I was coming on too strong."

Not in his world. "Don't worry." He smacked her ass playfully. "Tonight, we're in charge, as soon as we're off the clock. Let's get this over with so we can cut out."

The first client, a vamp, was raising hell in the reception area. He bared his fangs at a female staffer. She made the sign of the cross using her forefingers.

"Wait." Zoe yanked on Stefin's shirt.

A little more and she'd pull it off him. Looking over, he smiled. "As much as I'm ready to play again, we don't have time for it now. Unfortunately, Becca expects us to work before we can leave for the evening."

"Yeah, I get that. Where are you and the guys taking me tonight?"

"Everywhere we can." Surely, that was obvious to her.

Taro and Anatol nodded.

Zoe made a frustrated noise. "I meant the place." Unease tightened her features. "Are we going back to the Crucible? Will they even allow that after what I — we — I did?"

"The owner said our next meal's on him." Anatol kissed Zoe's knuckles. "We really livened up the place."

"That we did." Stefin settled his mouth on her ear. "However, the Crucible is kindergarten next to where we'll be going tonight."

"Guys." The staffer leaned away from the amorous vamp. "Got a sec?"

Zoe grabbed Stefin's arm. "Where?"

He pried her fingers off him and chucked her chin. "You'll see." He spoke to the staffer. "Coming."

Stefin made a beeline for the vamp, followed by Anatol and Taro.

Wanting an answer, Zoe followed.

Someone grabbed her arm.

"Walk, don't run." Constance spoke softly. "Play it cool. Guys like that."

Zoe got in her face. "Where are they taking me?"

MJ joined them. "A place like no other." Adding nothing to her cryptic comment, she fled.

Becca hurried past and mouthed 'have fun' over her shoulder.

Heather smiled sweetly. "I'm so happy for you."

"Me, too." Constance released Zoe's arm and raced after the others.

Zoe drooped against the wall. There wasn't a way in hell she could play it cool when she'd behaved so idiotically last night—riding Taro like a pony, trying to pull off Stefin's cock, wanting to use Anatol's dreadlocks like a rope, using her power to imprison them so she could attack. She fought an urge to vaporize herself. At least she hadn't confessed her love. If she had, the guys wouldn't be here today. They certainly wouldn't be taking her to wherever the fuck they were going.

Stefin backed toward a treatment room, gesturing for Anatol and Taro to follow. They held the vamp in a head lock. He squirmed worse than a freshly harvested soul, feverishly trying to sink his fangs into them.

Taro whacked him. "Stop that."

"No." Spittle dripped off his teeth. "It's my last chance to enjoy myself before you guys torture me."

"Treat you." Anatol shook the vamp roughly.

"Zoe." Stefin looked over. "We're about ready."

She joined them in the room.

Anatol and Taro scuffled with the vamp. He tried his damndest to get free, even morphing into a bat. Taro smacked him from the ceiling to the floor. Anatol stepped on a leathery wing until the vamp assumed human form. He bitched, clawed and snapped his teeth, refusing to surrender. A typical reaction for a new client. Everyone wanted to change for the better, until the time came to do so. Then it was *fuggedaboutit*. Similar to mortals who were eager to get into shape until they actually got to the gym.

As a rule, Zoe didn't have much patience. Tonight was worse than usual. The more the vamp struggled, the longer the shift would be.

She was already running on fumes. "Okay, that's it," she growled. "Settle down or else."

He jumped to his feet and displayed his fangs. They were longer than a saber tooth tiger's.

Like that was going to scare her. She rammed her heel into his foot and slammed her shoulder into his midsection.

Howling, he flailed his arms to regain his balance but couldn't. His back hit the table. His feet tangled with the furniture legs. He dropped like a rock.

Taro yanked him up, tossed him on the table and secured his restraints.

"About tonight." Zoe backhanded Stefin's hard belly. "Where. Are. We. Going?"

He gave her a wicked grin. "Don't you mean where are we taking you? Literally."

Being blunt wasn't getting her anywhere. Zoe eased into him, ran her fingers down his shirt buttons and made goo-goo eyes as Heather always did with Daemon. "Please tell me?"

He leaned so close their lips almost touched. If she'd had a soul, it would have sung. Now she had him.

"No." Stefin straightened. "It's a surprise." He eyed her curiously. "Having second thoughts about tonight?"

Those would probably come tomorrow if she had another blackout. "Can you at least keep an eye on me while we're out? Make sure I don't drink too much?"

"Not to worry. You won't make one move unless we allow it. Right, guys?"

Taro and Anatol gave two thumbs-up.

Stefin swatted her ass playfully. "Tonight, it's our show."

That didn't make things a whole lot better as far as Zoe was concerned. Even though she was dying to jump their bones and have them maul hers, she needed some insight into what was going down. After what had happened at the Crucible, she didn't want to behave stupidly again, and not because they'd dump her. She'd learned they weren't picky when it came to a woman's conduct.

Zoe's concern was for herself. She wanted to act like a winner, not a loser or a lunatic.

According to Constance, that meant playing it cool. Fat chance that would happen if she didn't know the program.

No matter how much she bugged MJ and Constance, neither would tell her what they knew. Becca was also uncharacteristically quiet, not that keeping her peace mattered. Each time they made eye contact, Becca blushed scarlet and hurried away without saying a word.

The shift couldn't have dragged more. Every freaking supernatural bitched about the treatments not working fast enough or being too brutal. Eventually, the whining became background noise to Zoe. She concentrated on having Stefin, Taro and Anatol's thick cocks in her mouth, cunt and anus, their hands roaming her boobs and ass, fingers stroking her clit.

She shivered.

"Hey!" The client underscored his outcry with a howl. A natural reaction, since he was a were. "Turn it off before you fucking kill me!"

Since they were overbooked tonight, Zoe had agreed to help a staffer with this dude. Unfortunately, she'd set the therapy lamp for ninety minutes, instead of fifty, the ideal time to build resistance to a full moon. Being exposed to so much light produced the opposite effect. Hair sprouted everywhere, even on his lips and tongue. He spit it out and wailed.

Anatol hurried into the room, followed by Stefin and Taro. They took one look at her screw-up and shook their heads.

Taro bumped her hip with his. "Bad, bad girl."

His teasing and the lovely ridge between his legs made her mouth water.

Stefin turned her around and pushed her gently to the door. "We'll take care of this while you get ready. We leave in ten minutes."

Before she could ask about their destination, MJ was in the hall. She gripped Zoe's wrist. "Let's go."

Zoe held back. "Where?"

They ended up in her office. Becca, Constance and Heather were already inside. However, there weren't any clothes or mirrors.

Zoe put distance between herself and them. "Don't tell me I'm supposed to show up nude." Being stripped bare when she was alone with the guys was one thing. They made her so loopy, she didn't worry about her appearance and at the Crucible, she'd been too wasted to care. They could have shaved her head and she wouldn't have noticed.

"Nope, you won't be nude." MJ braided Heather's hair. "Way better than that."

Zoe made a face. "Skinned?"

Constance laughed. Heather turned ashier than usual. Becca pinched her nose.

MJ's eyes rounded. "Wow, you have real trust issues, don't you?"

"Do I?" Zoe paced. "The lovely people of Salem hanged me for selling my soul to Satan for a guy I didn't get. Seems I forgot to read the fine print about free will and all that crap. So, yeah, I have a little trust problem."

"Perfectly understandable and we'll never screw with your head." Becca shot MJ an admonishing look. "Isn't that right, MJ?"

"Not a chance." Fake innocence shone on her face.

Something popped.

From experience, Zoe looked down. Her clothing hadn't changed. She didn't get it.

Heather cooed. "This is nice."

She wore a brutal black corset that stopped beneath her naked boobs and dipped to the blonde curls between her legs. Her boots had heels so high it looked as if she was walking on her toes, like a ballerina. Leather slave bracelets hugged her biceps.

Zoe spoke to MJ. "Did you goof up and do her instead of me?"

"Oh, no." Heather giggled. "I'm modeling this for you, like MJ and I do for each other so we know what to wear to clubs."

"You like?" MJ swept her hand, taking in Heather's full length. "Or would you prefer something different?"

"Like clothes? Sure."

"Sorry, no can do." A new pop sounded.

This time, Heather was in a black thing that consisted of leather strips which barely crisscrossed over her nipples and mound.

"Turn around." MJ made a circle with her finger. "Show her the back."

"That's okay. I'd rather not see it." Zoe didn't want to be critical, but… "No way am I wearing that. Are the guys taking me to a BDSM club?"

The ladies exchanged glances. MJ spoke first. "Not exactly."

This was nuts. "Then what exactly?"

"Ah, guys?" Becca tapped her watch. "We don't have a lot of time before she has to take off."

MJ nodded and spoke to Zoe. "You'll just have to trust me."

A pop louder than the others rang through the room.

Zoe gasped. Calling her dressed wasn't a term anyone would use. Her black leather bra didn't have cups. Gold rings hung from her naked nipples. How, she hadn't a clue. She didn't feel the metal piercing her skin. Dangling from the two rings were thin gold chains. They snaked down her torso to her panties, if she could call them that. There wasn't a crotch. Her ass was bare. Leather bands hugged her hips, ran between her butt cheeks and exhibited her bush. Another gold ring hung from it, attached to her labia.

Leather bands circled her wrists. Each sported a gold ring. A collar fit her throat so snugly it tightened each time she swallowed. Her hair hung free, not that it covered much except for the hickey Taro had left on her shoulder and the puncture wounds from the vamp. The only parts on her that were clothed were her legs. She wore thigh-high leather boots, also in black, that laced in front and had spike heels. Not bad for footwear. The rest though…

She spoke to the group. "All of you know where the guys are taking me tonight. Even if you don't want to tell me where that is, please say it's going to be dark there."

If it wasn't, she'd freak looking like this.

The ladies exchanged a glance.

"Part of it will be." Constance spoke to the others. "Right?"

Becca lifted her shoulders. "Never been there."

The others shook their heads.

Not good enough. "Where is there?"

Heather hugged her. "Stop worrying. You look incredibly hot. Better than I did when I wore basically the same thing to Whatever Goes."

"Anything Goes." MJ grinned. "A really cool BDSM club for satyrs and their nymphs."

"Yeah, Heather mentioned it before." Disquiet and excitement swirled through Zoe. "Is that where the guys are taking me tonight?" If so, she couldn't figure out how they'd get in if they didn't have hooves, horns and a tail. The horns and tails they could manage, if they reverted to their pure demon form, but the rest could be a problem unless they used their powers to morph into satyrs. She spoke to Heather, "You actually dressed like I am now?"

"Not totally, but close. I got a ton of compliments on my outfit from the satyrs and the nymphs."

MJ slung her arm over Heather's shoulders. "You wouldn't believe how popular she is. The guys always get a little rowdy. After the dust settles, she heals their injuries."

"How rowdy does it get?" It couldn't be worse than the Crucible.

"Doesn't matter." Constance adjusted her turban. "The boys aren't taking you to Anything Goes."

"Then where?" Zoe tapped her foot, hoping to show her frustration that way rather than smoking and messing up her do. It worked, except no one answered her question. She shook from tension and concern. Her nipple rings shimmied. "Come on, you have to tell me or at least provide a clue."

"Zoe!" Stefin.

Constance's eyes glittered. "Your Master's voice. A little advice, don't keep him or the others waiting."

MJ shoved Zoe into the hall, the same as she'd done earlier.

After steadying herself, Zoe didn't know what to do. She was the only one out here, the guys nowhere in sight.

Constance leaned against the jamb. "They're in the storage closet."

A hand snaked around that door. Stefin's, given the tat. He curled his finger, gesturing for her to join him.

Zoe toddled down the hall, rickety in her heels.

"Wait!"

Despite Becca's shout, Zoe took two more steps before she could halt. Breathing hard, she looked over. Part of her hoped Becca would order her to get dressed. Another part needed this decadence so badly she was ready to slug Becca if she interfered. "Why?"

Becca held up her finger for quiet and faced the closet. "Stefin, Anatol, Taro. You take care of Zoe tonight. Do. You. Hear. Me? If you don't, I'll have your balls. Understand?"

Dead freaking silence.

Zoe couldn't imagine what had gotten into Becca. She was going to ruin tonight for her. She shouldn't have said anything to them.

"Don't worry, we will." Stefin had never sounded more sincere.

Anatol chimed in. "Promise."

"You bet." Taro.

Becca hugged Zoe harder than Heather had, both of them hanging on, despite her hot demon skin. "Kick ass. Show them what you got. What they can't live without because you are the finest woman and demon they've ever known."

Tears stung Zoe's eyes. "Thanks. Wish me luck."

"Screw that. You don't need it."

Buoyed by Becca's words and the guys' promise to watch over her, Zoe fairly danced to the closet.

The supplies were gone, replaced by a floor carpeted in red velvet and walls made from accordion grates, the kind old buildings have in the elevators.

Oddest thing she'd ever seen.

Even stranger, Zoe hadn't been the only one getting dressed, or rather undressed.

Stefin, Anatol and Taro had ditched their shirts, pants and footwear for black combat boots that laced up the front like hers. They wore what looked to be tights, also black. The part in front was cut out to reveal their meaty cocks and pendulous balls. Whips hung from the leather belts around their waists. Each sported a red cape that draped their shoulders and backs, but left their chests bare.

Zoe grabbed the doorknob for support. "Someone's been reading *Story of O*." If she had to guess, she'd say tonight was about dominance, submission, punishment and pleasure.

They stared at the delicate curls between her legs, blatantly displayed by her crotchless thong, and her boobs exposed by her bra without cups. Her nipples couldn't get any tighter. Nor did she believe their cocks could have grown longer or stiffer.

Her legs threatened to give out at what awaited. Her pussy pulsed as if to say, "Oh, yeah."

Stefin curled his finger, wanting her in the closet.

They couldn't be staying in there. There wasn't enough room for what she required.

She stepped inside. The door slammed on its own, Zoe flinched. Rather than the overhead fixture raining its yellowish light on them, the walls and grates glowed red.

Amazing, kind of pretty, too. "Where are we going?"

The enclosure plummeted so fast, the descent snatched her breath. Everyone's hair flew up. The space grew warmer.

That meant only one thing. Zoe could scarcely breathe. "Are we going to Hell?"

Stefin winked. Anatol grinned, making a dimple.

Taro pressed his cheek to hers. "The second circle."

Lust.

Chapter Eleven

Zoe grabbed the grill. "Stop this thing. *Now*."

That wasn't the reaction Stefin had expected. Her soft purr or coo, followed by her thanking him, was more what he had in mind.

She rattled the grates. "I mean it. *Stop*."

They dropped faster. The temperature rose quickly. Before she burned herself on the increasingly hot metal, Stefin pried her fingers away and held them. "What's wrong?"

"Are you kidding me? Have you lost your mind?"

Although she'd directed her question to him, Taro and Anatol, no one answered.

Zoe yanked her hands from Stefin and smacked his chest. "Do you have a death wish?"

He rubbed his slapped pec. "Not since I became immortal. But if I did want to die, I'm sure you'd be happy to finish me off." He didn't much like her pissy mood. "What is the matter with you?"

Where had his sweet submissive Zoe gone?

She ground her fist into her forehead. "We can't go back to Hell."

"Why not?"

"Wait." Taro cupped her face. "Is there a bounty on you?"

Stefin hadn't considered that. He figured Satan had expelled Zoe because she'd been such a pain in the ass, like she was being now. If she'd escaped and had been hiding out, that would present a problem.

He shoved Taro aside and held her chin. "What did you do?"

She gave him a look that said he'd grown two heads and neither had a brain. "Nothing. You guys have." She wrenched free. "I saw your files, remember? If you defy Satan by putting as much as a toe into Hell, he'll lock you up forever. No parole. It'll be bread and water time. Hard labor. Endless music from the Bieb. Maybe even the Carpenters." Her lower lip quivered. "I can't let that happen."

Stefin didn't want that, either, though her reaction and coming tears did intrigue him. "Why not?"

She shook her head and turned away. Her shoulders trembled.

So much tenderness welled within Stefin, he feared crying but didn't. Wouldn't. During life, sissy emotions could have gotten him killed. In Hell, he would have been put on display and ridiculed. The peer pressure down there was obscene. He gathered her to him and stroked her hair. Few things were as silky. Her back was the same, her ass plush and cushiony beyond compare. The furrow between her butt cheeks couldn't have been warmer. Her anus was a delight too.

"Holy hell," she growled. "What are you doing?"

"Don't you know? Honestly?" He ground his cock against her pussy. "No BS now."

"You're impossible."

That was the pot calling the kettle black. She squirmed, not remotely as turned on as he was. Baffled at her reaction, he went for broke and rubbed her clit.

She moaned throatily but pushed him away.

Stefin collided with Taro, who bumped into Anatol.

"You're all about to fuck yourselves royally." She kicked the grating. "And the only thing you can think about is sex."

Anatol looked at her blankly. "That's not true."

Zoe gestured to their rigid cocks.

Stefin figured he should point out the obvious. "They're always this way,"

She barked a laugh then sobbed. "Please don't do this. I'm begging you." Tears streamed down her cheeks.

Her worry and sorrow transfixed him. During his years on Earth, no one had ever wept over him, not even when he'd been a young boy. Once he'd landed in Hell, everyone had been a hard-ass, the same as him, all trying to out-macho the other.

In his entire existence, he hadn't known a kind word, a gentle touch, nor had anyone given a crap about his welfare. He'd been a lost cause from day one. Completely alone.

Zoe sniffed. "Don't put yourselves at risk for me. I'm not worth it."

Nothing could have been further from the truth. For her, Stefin would have chanced reincarnation and being born to conservative parents who'd send him to Bible camp and an ultra-restrictive university that banned keg parties and panty raids.

He hadn't known her feelings ran so deep and needed her to tell him more. "Why?"

Zoe loved them too much. She'd never recover if they got caught and Satan took them away from her for eternity. She would rather ask MJ for a wish that they fall in love with another demon who'd keep them in New Orleans, far from Hell. Their affection for another woman would destroy Zoe, but she'd prefer to have them safe rather than risk their futures for one night.

This evening was merely about fun, not commitment. Becca's pep talk had been nice, but no more than a friend's affection speaking, not reality.

Zoe wrapped her arms around herself.

The guys shifted their weight. Smacking sounds followed.

She guessed they were punching each other's biceps.

Anatol muttered in French, "Cretins. Say something to her."

"Us?" Taro made a mocking noise. "How about you turn on the charm, Mr. Finesse?"

"Zoe." Stefin lifted her chin so she'd meet his gaze. "We're not in any danger."

Tell that to her battered hope and sinking spirit. "Don't lie to me. I can stand anything but to have you lie."

"I'm not." He thumbed away her tears. "Have you ever been to the second circle?"

He couldn't be serious. The moment she'd discovered how Satan had tricked her, Zoe had hounded his sorry ass, irritating him like a rash that wouldn't go away. She'd bitched about everything nonstop to show him what Hell really was. "No. I was too busy with other stuff. But I've heard rumors that it's hot. Figuratively."

Anatol stroked her arm. "Has the best night spots ever."

She hadn't known that. "Like places to party?"

"You have no idea." Taro pressed her hand to his chest.

His heated skin drained away her apprehension faster than sucking down a gallon of booze. "Doesn't Satan go to them?"

"Hell, no. He's a special snowflake." Stefin rolled his eyes. "Same as the politicians, bankers and Wall Streeters who are down there. They have their own places, gated from the rest of us plebs." He stroked the furrow between her cheeks.

Too much delight whisked through her. She shot to her toes.

He explored her anus.

Hard lust replaced her other emotions. He should have had a PhD in foreplay.

Anatol pushed Stefin's hand from her.

Zoe frowned.

"*Chérie*, even if Satan didn't stay in the elite spots, the second circle is bigger than this universe."

Taro nodded. "And all the others combined."

"There are places in the second circle Satan has never known about." Stefin leaned against the grating, made a face and promptly pulled away. "He's a busy guy, right? He can't possibly keep his fingers in everything, no matter what he claims."

"'Claims' is right." Taro got a sour look. "Everything that comes out of his mouth is a damn lie."

Zoe couldn't dispute that. "Tell me about it."

Gingerly, Stefin touched his back.

She reached for him. "Did you burn yourself?"

He stiffened. "Nope. Nothing to fret about, especially in the second circle. We'll be safe."

She wanted to believe it but couldn't help worrying. "What about his spies and his army of snitches?"

"Everyone has a price." Stefin shrugged. "You just have to know what it is, negotiate it down to prove you're the man then pay through the nose."

"You actually did that?"

They nodded.

"With cash?"

They exchanged looks. Stefin shook his head first. "Our powers."

"*What?*"

"Take it easy. We had to give some of them away. They'll build again in a month or two. No biggie."

To her, it was monumental. She wanted to hug her guys to show how much she loved them, but didn't dare do so. This was about nothing more than having a good time. "What is this particular nightspot we're going to? What's it like?"

The closet elevator halted abruptly and bounced gently from its sudden landing. Zoe's hair fell on her shoulders, Stefin's and Anatol's tumbled to theirs. Taro's locks grazed his forehead.

"You're about to see what's in store." Stefin gestured to the door.

It swung open on its own and ushered in sulfur and musk scents rich with wickedness.

She could barely breathe.

Fires flared on the brimstone landscape. The light tried to eat away shadows too numerous to count. Something skittered within the darkness, first on two legs then all fours and disappeared before she could identify what it was. An orange-reddish glow filled the sky. Silhouetted against it were craggy mountains. Lava flowed from the peaks. Smoke plumes rose everywhere.

This was way different from Satan's digs. He'd fashioned his places to resemble Trump's Mar-a-Lago, Marie Antoinette's Palace of Versailles and the Taj Mahal. His off-season digs weren't as opulent but would have made a billionaire weep with envy.

For centuries, Zoe had been stuck in that splendor as a scullery maid and a pest.

Eager to see the real Hades, she rushed from the enclosure.

Stefin hauled her back in. "Tonight, we give the orders. You don't make one move on your own. You submit."

No way would she argue with that game plan. They'd proven themselves by carefully choosing this place and bribing the snitches. Like most guys, they may have thought about nothing but sex, but they weren't fools. More importantly, they'd made certain she'd be safe even before Becca had issued her warning. Excitement and adoration pumped through Zoe. Her stomach fluttered. "Whatever you say, mister."

Stefin affected his most imperious pose. "Master."

Charmed by his bold machismo, she nodded submissively.

He held out his hand. Taro gave him a long gold chain. Stefin ran it through her collar ring, those on her nipples and the one dangling from her pussy.

No one had to tell Zoe he was going to lead her around like his trophy slave.

She shivered happily.

"We do the talking." Stefin gave her a stern look. "You keep quiet."

"That's right." Taro ground his erect cock into her ass and nuzzled her neck.

She sagged against him.

Anatol played with her nipple rings and thumbed the tips. Each stroke made her crazy for more. She pulled away from Taro and slumped into Anatol.

"Make sure you obey our every command." Anatol's lilt bore a hard edge. "Or there will be hell to pay."

"Oh, yeah?" She grinned. "Tell me."

"It's show time." Stefin pried the others away and wrapped the chain around his hand. "Keep up with me. I don't want these links to pull tight."

"Neither do we." Taro drew his whip across her ass. The leather tails dangled over her thighs.

She expected he and the others would punish her with their whips or riding crops, pulling cry after cry from her, pain and pleasure mingling to create one breathtaking experience.

Goosebumps rose on her arms. A pulse ticked deep within her pussy.

Stefin stepped out onto the landscape. It was eerily quiet then sounds surged toward them, the noise level greater than a hundred freight trains. Fires sputtered, rocks exploded, something unearthly let out a piercing shriek.

Blaring music drowned out everything else. The tune mingled hard rock and extreme metal, the bass so loud it shook the ground.

Zoe bobbed her shoulders to the beat.

Stefin regarded her, one eyebrow arched.

She stilled, properly tamed.

His cock plumped even more, the skin so taut she feared it would burst.

Taro strode past and led the way, his cape flapping in the sweltering breeze. Stefin and Zoe followed. Anatol brought up the rear. Heated rocks crunched beneath their boots. However, the extreme temperature didn't singe the leather or bother her feet.

The bass grew louder. A vocalist shrieked his lyrics like Steven Tyler of Aerosmith always did, unless it was him. Zoe hadn't heard that he'd died, but who knew? He surely looked older than Death.

They approached a cavernous area carved into a mountainside, a humungous arch at its entrance. Male and female demons, trussed up in chains, dangled from the structure. Other demons crawled over those naked bodies and sucked cocks, licked cunts or boobs and penetrated every orifice.

Those on the receiving end writhed in pleasure.

Anatol pressed his mouth to her ear. "That's the riffraff who couldn't afford the cover charge. They hang out here, listening to the music."

They looked as if they couldn't have cared less about the rough beat. One after the other reached climax and moaned heartily. As they drifted down from pleasure, the orgy paused for a moment then they were back at it, wailing like the world had ended or their next orgasm was near.

She wondered if they ever got tired doing the same thing repeatedly, without a break. Even carnal activities grew boring after a while. She supposed that's why this was Hell. No rest for the wicked. No chocolate, either. She'd found that out early on.

They crossed the archway. Sultry air delivered an odor scented heavily from sex.

Anticipation weakened Zoe so much her bones might as well have dissolved.

The guys led her deeper into the space. Lewd, carnal images decorated the walls, ceiling and floor, all life size and carved into the stone. Or not. One image came to life, the lovers in it humping like crazy. The one next to it also came alive followed by another and…

She stopped at the show.

The chain grew taut between her and Stefin. He tugged it.

Zoe couldn't budge. She pointed at the wall. Not because Stefin had told her to keep quiet. Too stunned to form words, she mouthed, 'What is that?'

Taro ran his whip over her stomach. "It's what happens when you try to sneak in without paying. You're trapped in stone forever, screwing around with the same babe you brought."

How romantic. Like full-on commitment. The ten-letter word that sent guys running. She studied Taro, trying to determine what he thought about forever after.

His face turned as red as his hair.

Zoe suspected it wasn't from the heat.

He averted his gaze and led them deeper into the space. Real demons replaced the stone ones and engaged in what came naturally, or unnaturally, on the ornate sofas, chairs, tables and rugs. Arms and legs stuck out at awkward angles, those limbs impossibly entwined.

And here she'd been worried about someone gawking at her. Every being in this place was so busy banging themselves crazy a nuclear explosion wouldn't have caught their attention.

She couldn't explore enough and stopped at a group whose hands and feet were chained to the wall. Many panted and writhed, close to orgasm. The second they were ready to peak, the demons arousing them stopped.

They wailed in protest, their agonized cries drowning out the music.

They must have done something pissing bad to be cheated out of a climax, in the second circle, no less. Could be they'd paid the cover charge using a bad check or a stolen credit card.

A tall blonde moaned pitifully. The demon tonguing her clit wouldn't let her come.

Zoe stopped dead, forgetting to follow the guys and to be quiet. "Rachel?"

Stefin growled. "Zoe."

"Wait." She pointed frantically. "I know the girl on the end. I was alive when she was. We were BFFs in Salem."

The guys glanced at each other.

"I gotta talk to her." Zoe was prepared to plead as she never had. "Please. I'm begging you."

"Go on." Stefin's frown softened. "But after that, you follow us."

She nodded obediently and hurried to the wall.

He followed close behind to keep the chain loose.

"Whoa." The demon at Rachel's feet put out his arm to keep Zoe away. "Wait your turn."

She seethed. "This is my turn." Smoke poured from her hair and shoulders. "Back off, got it?"

Taro smacked his whip against the guy's shoulder. "Move. Now."

Anatol joined them. "Or we'll make you."

Zoe loved them and Stefin for being so considerate. "Thanks." She rushed to her friend. "Rach?"

Perspiration dampened her face and hair. Panting, she struggled to part her lids. Once she had, recognition lit her eyes. "Zo?"

Zoe grinned hard enough to make her cheeks hurt. "Yeah. I didn't know you were here. How'd you end up in this place? Hell, I mean."

"Aw, crud, it's a long story."

"I don't mind."

Stefin muttered something beneath his breath. Zoe patted his belly to calm him. When that didn't work, she stroked his rod.

Rachel watched the exchange with growing interest.

Zoe snapped her fingers to get Rachel's attention. "Go on, tell me."

She looked uneasy. "Remember your guy?"

"What guy?" Stefin crowded Zoe.

His jealousy over anyone except Taro and Anatol surprised her. She liked it. "Some dude I knew when I was alive. Ancient history." She spoke to Rachel. "Yeah, I remember." She'd spent more than three hundred years trying to forget the prick. Even now, his indifference stung. "What about him?"

Rachel bit her bottom lip. "I fell for him, too."

A month ago, that would have sent Zoe into a tailspin, her fury followed by endless despair. Stefin, Anatol and Taro had changed that. She shrugged. "Hey, you're entitled. He was the hottest dude in the village. His muscles went from here to tomorrow."

Rachel giggled. "I loved watching him make horseshoes. Why blacksmiths ever died out is beyond me."

"No kidding. You and he hooked up for a while?"

"Would I be here if we had?"

Zoe sensed what was coming. "Satan screwed you over, too?"

"Big time. Something about free will and Ebenezer using it to avoid me, even after I'd sold my soul to get him."

What a freaking scam the Prince of Darkness had going. The ghouls on Wall Street had nothing on him.

"Ebenezer?" Stefin choked on a laugh.

Taro and Anatol snickered.

Rachel took them in, tarrying on their balls and cocks. The flames in her eyes danced. "Your new posse?"

Zoe puffed up with pride. "Masters."

The guys stopped laughing. Untold need filled their gazes.

Zoe twirled her slave chain and bobbed to the savage beat. "Catch up with you later, 'kay?"

Rachel smiled. "Don't be a stranger. By the way, dynamite outfit."

Zoe struck a pose like a Victoria's Secret model, pure sass and sexy innocence. "Thanks. My Masters like it." She spoke to them. "Don't you?"

Stefin's leer nearly set her on fire.

He pulled her into his arms and slanted his mouth over hers, his kiss deep, wet and fucking hard. He gripped her ass and ground his cock into her cunt as he enjoyed her mouth, his tongue filling her to the point that not even a whimper could escape.

Rachel sighed. "Oh, yeah."

Taro took Zoe next, her back to his front. He slipped one arm around her waist and used the other to turn her face to his. Once he'd captured her mouth and drove his tongue inside, he palmed her nipples and gently tugged the rings.

She weakened, giddy from desire.

He toyed with the ring on her cunt then concentrated on her clit. His first stroke pulled a pleased gasp from her. The next threatened to send her over the edge.

Before he could do so, Anatol lifted Zoe.

She wrapped her legs around his lean hips, her damp pussy pressed against his groin, arms circling his shoulders. They made out like Tasmanian devils. The noises that poured from them were outrageous and beautiful, revealing their passion.

The room lurched. Her lips felt bruised. If nothing other than this happened tonight, she'd still be eternally grateful for their attention and fierce desire.

Anatol ended their kiss and released her. She wavered.

The demon was back at Rachel's feet.

Zoe clamped his shoulder to steady herself. "I'm not sure I can walk just yet. Give me a minute."

"No more than that." Stefin's cock defied gravity and pointed at her. "Too much to do."

Her blood sang from impossible need. "Oh, yeah?"

"You have no idea." Taro squeezed her ass.

Anatol stroked her bush. "We'll show you."

Chapter Twelve

Zoe might have been a demon and a born hell-raiser, but Anatol knew she had a lot to learn when it came to carnal pleasure. Her surprise at the vanilla things she'd seen down here proved how innocent she was.

Tonight would be like no other in her existence. He wanted her to experience ultimate delight without recrimination or heartache. He hoped she'd learn to trust guys.

When her friend had mentioned Ebenezer, embarrassment had changed Zoe from sexy to uncertain. With a name like his, she should have ground her shoe in his face, or better yet, squashed his balls. The prick was a blacksmith to boot. As far as Anatol was concerned, that made him an uneducated savage, not good enough for his Zoe.

He stilled at thinking she was his, uncertain where his possessiveness had come from.

She leaned into his hand.

He hadn't realized he'd been stroking her clit, giving her pleasure, behaving as a man would when that was his sole purpose in life. He slipped two fingers into her cunt to prepare her for the wild hours ahead.

Zoe moaned. She grabbed his dreadlocks and yanked him into her. Her kiss was wicked as hell and heavenly, too. Their tongues did a slow, sexy waltz.

Need overwhelmed him. He hauled her as close as he could, which wasn't nearly enough, and wanted to take her here, now.

Stefin grumbled. "Enough."

Maybe for him. Anatol was just getting started. His passion erupted as it hadn't since he'd lost Gigi. Zoe, his Zoe, did that to him. He tore his mouth free and spoke to Stefin. "Get lost."

"My thoughts exactly. For you." He pulled Anatol away from her and swung him to the side.

Once Anatol regained his balance, he bunched his shoulders, ready for battle.

Stefin did the same.

Those around them fell silent, waiting for the fight.

A passing demon shook his head. "Bad move."

He had a point. A brawl would bring the bouncers here. The rules were strict — everyone was supposed to make love, not war. Any demon who didn't obey was tossed out and never allowed to return.

Anatol gave Stefin the finger. Thankfully, vulgar hand gestures and verbal obscenities weren't prohibited.

Ignoring him, Stefin grabbed Zoe's chain. "Let me know when you're ready to go, and for the nth time, keep up."

"Please." Taro stroked her hair. "If you don't, we'll never get to the good part."

Anatol could scarcely wait any longer. What they'd planned for her was so damn awesome.

Zoe had trouble containing her elation. This night was pure wonder. Not only filled with sin as she'd expected, but Stefin and Anatol had behaved like men in love, ready to fight over her. As Taro had done with the demon at the Crucible. How freaking sweet was that?

Happy tears threatened until she recalled that this evening was merely about sex, not friendship or her guys' emotional needs that only she could satisfy. There were a zillion babes here, each aching for pleasure. Most were built and far better looking than she would ever be even after a gazillion wishes from MJ or countless potions from Becca's mom. These ladies were perfect naturally and would be more than willing to give Anatol, Taro and Stefin whatever they wanted. Being demons, her guys wouldn't walk the straight and narrow forever, no matter how much she would have liked them to do so. Better remember that.

She looked over at Rachel. "Later."

Rachel studied Taro, Anatol and Stefin's assets. Lust colored her cheeks, making them as rosy as her pouty lips. "You bet." She made a low, wanting sound, similar to a female beast on the hunt.

"Let's go." Zoe hotfooted away and gestured for her guys to follow before Rachel got any ideas. Like throwing herself at them as she'd probably done with Ebenezer. It was a miracle he hadn't fallen for her. She had an angel's face and boobs as big as cantaloupes. Maybe he'd been into guys.

Stefin yanked her chain. "Hold it."

Realizing her faux pas, Zoe stopped. She batted her eyelashes at him. "Sorry, Master."

He looked torn between bitching and laughing.

Zoe blew him a kiss.

Stefin broke into a broad grin. He shook it off and leaned down to her. "No more delays."

"Hey, you call the shots. I obey, as I should." She affected her submissive pose, totally ready for what would come next.

They left the section where Rachel had been. The music faded. Replacing it was a steady drone that grew in intensity and blocked sounds from crackling fires and bursting rocks. Sexual fragrances were denser here than they'd been in the last place, the sulfur so intense she couldn't quite catch her breath.

She and her guys approached a narrow tunnel. An orangey glow brightened the other end. The previous hum evolved into countless conversations punctuated by numerous shouts.

Taro, Stefin and Anatol strode faster.

Zoe trotted to keep up.

They entered a gargantuan area dominated by a stadium that seated demons in the thousands. There was a full crowd tonight. Vendors crisscrossed the aisles like worker bees and sold their wares — booze for everyone, steaks for the guys, chocolate for the ladies.

Zoe couldn't believe it. Satan had said the dark treat wasn't available down here in any fucking place. Never in her existence had she met such a total dick.

One young woman had stuffed so much candy into her mouth, her cheeks puffed out like a chipmunk's. If she kept that up, she'd be prime material for the third circle. Gluttony.

A stage materialized on the stadium field. A wooden frame dominated the platform, chains and manacles on each side. Behind the uppermost seats were huge TV screens. Cameras zoomed in on the frame.

Her guys dashed to it, Zoe in tow.

She got a funny feeling she was this evening's entertainment. They were going to play with her on the stage while everyone watched.

Zoe stopped and shrank back. All eyes turned to her. The din quieted.

She broke out in a cold sweat, part apprehension at how she looked and what she lacked physically, part excitement at the coming pleasure.

Stefin tugged on her chain.

Anatol gave her a small shove from behind.

She wobbled so much, she looked like she was twerking and far less gracefully than Miley Cyrus. Zoe halted at the brief stairway that led to the platform. It looked taller than Mount Everest. Climbing those steps the normal way wasn't in the equation. Her legs were too weak. She'd have to crawl.

Stefin swept her into his arms.

The crowd roared in approval, the sounds deafening.

He let her down on the platform.

She clung to him and motioned for Taro and Anatol to join them.

The spectators complained.

Zoe didn't give a crap. She hung on to her guys, feeling safer with them than she ever had with anyone else.

Stefin ran his knuckles down her cheek. "Was the stadium a bad idea? Is it too much?"

His question was so sweetly naïve she wanted to laugh but didn't dare. She'd cut out her tongue before making fun or humiliating him and the others. They'd meant well, wanting to give her a rocking good time. Given how her desire kept building, they probably understood her better than she knew herself. "This is epic. You couldn't have chosen a better place. But how about me? How do I look?"

Stefin wrapped her in a bear hug. "Beautiful."

"And hot." Taro pulled her into his arms.

"Even better than that." Anatol swept her away from the others and into him. "Good enough to eat. Which we will."

Compliments fueled by lust, not love. Their generous praise still moved Zoe, because they cared enough to make her feel pretty and wanted. No man had ever done that before. Certainly not Ebenezer or Satan.

Zoe didn't need those losers. She was a different person now, ready for anything. "Let's give these demons a damn good show."

Stefin secured her wristbands to the chains on the frame.

The audience thundered their delight.

Anatol clamped manacles around her boots and tugged the links, forcing Zoe to spread her thighs widely.

Taro grabbed the chain that dangled from the top and ran it through the ring on her collar.

When they finished, she couldn't move an inch to the right, left, forward or backward. She was fully theirs.

Taro played with her nipple rings, coaxing an unholy gasp from her.

Spectators whistled and shouted.

"Hey, Taro!" Several female demons waved at him then tossed their crotchless panties on the stage. One fell on his shoulder.

He brushed it off and ignored them.

For that alone, Zoe would always adore him.

He grabbed her bra cups and yanked them apart. The leather tore, leaving her more exposed than she had been, proving she was his and the others' plaything, their sexual slave.

The onlookers pumped their fists and stomped their feet.

Taro eased into her. He touched the ring in her labia then worked her clit.

Dazzling pleasure ripped through her and coaxed new moisture from her pussy. Her head fell back. The damn thing was too heavy to keep up.

Someone cupped her ass and squeezed. Impossible to tell whether it was Stefin or Anatol. Both were gifted lovers.

Taro's face went red from lust then darkened to maroon in what looked like frustration. He dropped his hand and stepped away.

A hush fell over the crowd. The audience glanced to the right or left rather than at her. Many craned their necks to see better even though the TV screens showed everything in lewd living color.

Her pussy was in close up. Moisture glistened on those curls, her channel damper than it had ever been. Her folds were plump and slick. The gold ring pierced them.

The audience let out delighted whoops.

Sounded somewhat similar to the villagers who'd attended her hanging.

Thankfully, this was far more pleasant.

Anatol, Stefin and Taro circled and drank her in, their whips swaying lazily at their sides. Stefin stopped in front and pushed her ruined bra away so no part hid her. Anatol and Taro paused behind. They dragged Zoe's crotchless thong over her hips, leaving nothing between them and her nudity. They trailed their fingers between her butt cheeks.

Tingles dashed up her spine and down her thighs. The magical feeling settled in her pussy. She wavered.

The guys were back on the prowl, egged on by the crowd.

"Do it!" A guy in front had shouted.

That same refrain raced through the onlookers who grew louder and wilder. Several bouncers shoved the men back into their seats to keep them from swarming the stage.

Lightheaded, Zoe tried to avoid the TV screens but couldn't. They broadcast her naked ass and her thong beneath it, as useless for protection as her hands were. If she'd been unfettered, she didn't know if she would have covered her butt, furry mound or small boobs. Probably none of the above. This was too addictive, enticing her to seek more.

Stefin stopped at her side. "Have you been bad?"

"Hell, yeah!" Several guys in the audience had shouted as one.

The women grinned obscenely.

Zoe couldn't manage more than a nod.

Stefin pulled his whip from his belt and flicked the thing. Snapping sounds brought thousands to their feet, their arms waving, feet stamping. Stefin gave them a sly grin and fit his mouth to Zoe's.

She stiffened in surprise then collapsed against him.

His strength and heat were a balm that dispelled the shitty things in her past. His kiss was tender and searching, everything she desired. Nearly all she required, if it hadn't been for her also wanting his love. She pushed her foolish longing aside and kissed him in worship and honor. He was her Master, as the others were.

Taro kissed her next, followed by Anatol, each unique and the man she wanted.

Finished, they gathered behind her.

Gulping air, she looked over. A hand, possibly Stefin's, turned her face to the screen, her ass still displayed on it.

Strangely enough, she found it easier to regard her physical imperfections than to meet hungry male gazes in the crowd. All her life, she'd coveted attention but had never gotten it. Now that she had a taste of what pretty girls got so easily, along with her guys' affection, she couldn't imagine what her days would be like when this was over, which it would be. Stefin, Anatol and Taro would eventually move on while she still yearned.

A wiser demon would have cut bait and fled the crappy fallout.

She couldn't. This moment and the few others she had with them would just have to do.

As one, the crowd leaned forward or stared at the TV screens. They quieted.

Boots tapped the platform, Stefin, Taro and Anatol positioning themselves.

Perspiration trickled down her temples and throat. Unappeased lust glutted her pussy. She needed their cocks for relief. Unable to stand the wait any longer, she jerked her chains, trying to get free.

The restraints held fast.

Jeers rose from the crowd. The noise surged then fell to a less rabid level. A whistling sound cut through the clamor.

The screen showed the whip flick her ass and curl around her hip. A surreal moment that stopped time.

But not the sting. It registered hugely.

Zoe wailed and didn't stop until her breath ran out. Once she'd sucked in more air, she screeched anew and drowned out the others' excited cries. She might have shouted again if not for warmth cascading through her. The heat turned her pain to astonishing pleasure.

She drooled.

Stefin pressed his cheek to hers. "Doing okay?"

"No." The screen showed several red marks on her ass. Wasn't enough. "More."

"More what?"

She tugged her chains. "This. The whip. The heat." She couldn't stop ranting. "I can do without the sting, but hey, what's ecstasy without a little agony?"

"If you say so."

He stepped back. The whip struck her ass.

She growled out obscenities and fought her bonds. They wouldn't move. She yelled.

The crowd fell silent.

Anatol brushed his lips over hers. "Are you all right? Stefin mouthed that you were, but he's a loon. What did you really tell him?"

Zoe panted. "For everyone to quit asking me questions and to freaking get on with this." Perspiration ran down her face. "Dammit, I want more," she shouted louder than the other noise. "Now."

The audience whistled and bellowed their approval.

Four additional times, Stefin, Anatol or Taro punished her. Not once did they do real harm. The pain receded and blossomed into wicked pleasure like none she'd ever experienced.

Figuratively whipped, Zoe fought for a full breath. Her knees sagged. If she wasn't careful, her arms would pop from their sockets given her weight pulling on them. She didn't give a fig. Needing to chill, she rested her head on her shoulder.

Anatol released her ankles, Stefin her wrists. She sagged into Taro. He slung her over his shoulder and paraded across the stage, squeezing her whipped ass.

Crude catcalls poured from the audience.

"My turn." A male demon raced to the stage. "But I want to fuck her."

The bouncer tossed him into the cheap seats.

Female demons laughed.

Zoe couldn't believe how crazy hot this was. No way could her guys top this.

Then again…

The frame disappeared. In its place stood a King Kong-size bed. Black fur served as the comforter.

Someone had definitely read *Story of O.*

Taro lowered Zoe to her feet rather than on the mattress and kept her from dropping to it.

Vendors rushed through the crowd, delivering their stuff quickly as they would when a show was about to start up again.

Zoe expected Stefin to crawl on the mattress first. Taro beat him to it, his cape spread beneath him, legs fully apart, hand holding his cock. It looked longer than her forearm and far more delectable. Even fatigued, she was willing to do the work to bring her guys satisfaction.

Drunken voices rose within the crowd. Feet pounded.

She didn't have to ask if it was show time. Zoe pulled off her thong, shrugged out of her bra and threw the items into the audience. Several guys crashed into each other to catch her things. Those who succeeded had to fight off the ones who hadn't.

The bouncers pulled everyone apart.

Wow. This is great. Like being a rock star. However, she had more important matters to consider.

Wearing a bold smile, she crawled onto Taro and straddled his powerful legs. He'd rested one hand beneath his head, which exposed the dark auburn hair in his pit. She trembled in delight.

The crowd grew increasingly rowdy. Something shifted the mattress. She looked over.

Stefin was behind her, Anatol to the side. Both their rods were raring to go.

The perfect picture for what they all wanted and she required.

Zoe brushed her lips over Taro's, an intimate tease for what would come. On her knees, she guided his cock to her opening. The ride down him was remarkably smooth and easy given how wet she was, completely primed for him. Watching her channel swallow his rod was one of the most beautiful sights she'd ever witnessed. The thrill in having his hard length opening and filling her was too fantastic for words.

The audience shouted something rude, crude or lewd. She wasn't certain about the particulars, nor did she care. What happened on this bed was the only thing that mattered.

Taro's full length filled her. Their curls mingled, auburn-black, black-auburn, the mixture awesome. She blew out a sigh.

Unwilling to keep Stefin, Anatol or herself from ultimate delight, she swept her mouth over Taro's and lifted her ass.

Stefin accepted her invitation readily, as she'd hoped, and touched his crown to her anus. She pushed her butt into him, wanting more. He used moisture from her pussy to lubricate her tightest opening and entered her. Carefully for him, quite tenderly, in fact.

She had to calm herself at having both passages filled. She was close to blasting off without help from either guy. No way could she allow that. They were her Masters. The men she'd always want in her life.

Willing to settle for now, she fought for control.

Anatol knelt next to her. He pushed his cape over his shoulders and lifted his cock in his palm, presenting his black, bold and beautiful sex as a Dom would to his submissive, expecting her to love it.

Eagerly, she tongued his shaft into her mouth and took him as deep as she could.

He let out an uninhibited grunt.

To her, that said he liked what she'd done.

Stefin burrowed his cock fully into her anus and happily ground his groin into her ass. His sex plumped to amazing proportions. Taro's did the same in her sheath, his rod so beefy she could barely contain the lovely thing. However, if he or the others had given her more, she would have gladly welcomed it.

Noise from the crowd filtered back into her consciousness. Spectators fought the bouncers, shoved them aside and surrounded the platform. Not for a better look, since the TV screens provided that, but for the sexual scents coming from her, Stefin, Taro and Anatol. Ambrosia to the damned.

Zoe had never felt as lucky or as desired.

Time to party hearty.

Chapter Thirteen

Taro knew he would never experience Heaven, but this came pretty damn close. Zoe was a wonder, her passion precisely what he'd wanted yet more than he'd hoped for. When they'd first entered the stadium, she'd surprised him by being concerned about how she came off to the crowd. Why, he couldn't imagine. Kick-ass didn't begin to describe her hellaciously fun personality. Beautiful was an inadequate word when it came to her features. Outstanding couldn't come close to defining her sweet little boobs.

They bobbed merrily from her gyrations. The rings on the tips glinted.

He drove his rigid pole deeper into her cunt and eased back so he could go at her again. She matched his movements with a dancer's grace and a sex fiend's lust. The whole enchilada.

He wasn't certain how he'd gotten so lucky. This was spooky good, making his hair stand on end, the electricity between them undeniable.

Tina Donahue

Despite Anatol's cock in her mouth, Zoe's breath spilled out on a delighted sigh.

Taro deliberately grunted in pleasure to let her know how much he enjoyed this. There wasn't a man or demon alive who could resist her velvety bod, her cunt's incredible tightness and heat, the way it molded to his shaft, holding it in her tender embrace. The pleasure she generated was nearly more than he could bear, though not enough to satisfy. He couldn't touch her enough, at last toying with her nipple rings and the one in her soft folds before he stroked her clit.

She shuddered. The flames in her eyes flashed with immeasurable joy.

He longed to give her more, to have her experience it all.

If she ceased to exist at this moment, Zoe wouldn't have any right to complain. At least she'd found a sliver of paradise. Not enough for her insatiable appetite when it came to her guys, but better than she'd expected.

The world receded, leaving her, Taro, Stefin and Anatol wrapped in hazy pleasure. They made gruff noises that told Zoe how much she pleased them.

Stefin pumped his shaft into her anus and coordinated each thrust with Taro's rod in her pussy, both guys intent on satisfying her. Anatol was the same, moving his hips in time to the others so his rod glided within her mouth but never slipped out.

Perspiration drenched them. They hauled in air. Desire, excitement, damnation and sex scented them and the bed. Zoe shivered in unrepentant glee. She wanted this to go on forever and fought their attempts to drive her to orgasm.

They held back, too, pausing frequently. Their chests heaved from their strained attempts to catch their breaths. Once they did, they were back at it, intensifying their efforts. As Zoe serviced Anatol's cock, he stroked her cheek. Stefin trailed kisses on her back while thrusting his heavy sex into her anus. Taro teased her nub and jerked his hips repeatedly to drive his rod even deeper within her sheath.

Feverish and wanting, Zoe surrendered what little control she'd maintained and enjoyed them like a nympho or a woman in love. She pushed her ass into Stefin's groin, ground her cunt against Taro's crotch and sucked Anatol as if he were the best-tasting treat ever, which he and the others definitely were.

The mattress shifted beneath everyone's weight. The springs protested and pinged loudly. Other sounds joined the racket. Low chants rose to thunderous shouts. The demons' chorus of "Now. Now. Now. *Now.*"

Anatol reached liftoff first. His cum spurted into Zoe's mouth. He bellowed his delight. Taro growled and groaned through gritted teeth, his face as red as the lava outside. Stefin lasted a second longer and came with her.

She matched his spirited howl.

The audience sprang to their feet, their applause wild. Some whistled shrilly. Others jumped up and down.

Stefin eased his cock from her. Anatol did, too. Weakened, she fell to the side, bummed that Taro's rod had slipped from her sheath.

He snuggled close, so did Stefin and Anatol. All held her tenderly.

She resisted sleep, the same as they did, these moments too precious to waste. The vendors approached, hawking steaks, chocolate and booze. Stefin threw back a shot of vodka. Taro indulged in whiskey. Anatol sipped his wine. Zoe abstained and stuffed herself with chocolate. Once the guys had slaked their thirst, they gorged on steaks, replenishing the fuel they'd burned.

Stuffed, they returned to carnal activities. This time, they chained Zoe to a single post, arms above her head, her ass to them. They used leather straps to punish her then sucked the marks they'd made, increasing her delight. Each took her twice more before she and they fell in an exhausted heap on the bed, limbs tangled, mouths hanging open, too tired to speak or move.

* * * *

A noise Zoe couldn't place drifted close and away then close and…

She woke, surprised she'd passed out and lay on the bed alone. After struggling to one elbow, she glanced behind her. Those seats were empty except for a few demons sprawled across them, most likely drunk. Many snored loudly.

Possibly the sound that awakened her.

Another noise intruded. It rose and fell, similar to whispered conversations.

Someone laughed throatily. Despite the deep timbre, the voice sounded closer to a female demon than a male one.

Zoe rolled over.

Stefin, Anatol and Taro sat at the platform edge, their backs to her. They were nude, their boots, tights and capes forgotten near the mattress. Babes surrounded them, each gorgeous and built, their hair and eyes in a rainbow of colors. A blonde massaged Stefin's tattooed shoulders. Two brunettes played with Anatol's dreadlocks. The demon next to Taro had hair as black as Zoe's. She stroked his arm. Everyone chatted and laughed quietly.

No one, especially her guys, looked her way.

Jealousy hit so hard she grew lightheaded. An urge rose within her to shove those interlopers off the platform, away from what belonged to her. She pushed to her knees but couldn't manage more than that.

Stefin's quiet laughter mingled with Taro and Anatol's, their happiness obvious. They were enjoying themselves and she had no right to interfere. They weren't even her friends but merely temporary lovers. Their time together over now.

That truth was in the way they'd so easily moved on to new conquests.

Unwilling to hang around and hope for a crumb, as she'd done with Ebenezer, Zoe grabbed a cape and wrapped it around her nudity. She hurried down the steps then stopped to turn back one last time.

No one noticed or cared that she'd left. A repeat of Halloween.

She dashed through the tunnel and reached the room where she and Rachel had talked. Rachel was still against the wall, sweating and swearing. The same demon refused to let her come.

"Hey." Zoe smacked his shoulder. "Do her right."

Flames rocketed in his eyes. "I am."

Typical guy. Clueless, selfish, a player when it came to women. "Let. Her. Come."

He swore beneath his breath and aroused Rachel fully this time.

After screeching her release, she sagged against the wall, her limbs trembling. "Fuck."

Zoe smiled, happy for her, even though her own frustration mounted. Luckily, smoke didn't pour from her hair and shoulders. Tears filled her eyes instead. "Keep doing her that way. That's what women want. Consistency. Trust. Someone to depend on."

"Zo?" Rachel struggled to keep her lids open. "What are you doing here? Where's your posse? That is your Masters? What happened?"

Everything and nothing, which made Zoe's answer too long to get into. She lifted her hand in farewell and rushed away. Far quicker than before, she passed through the section with the writhing lovers then the one where the stoners were still humping and finally the arch were the riffraff dangled. All lost in their own world and pleasure. She held the cape tightly to her throat and retraced the path she and the guys had taken.

A creature darted through the shadows, this one on a single arm and two legs that gave it a weird gait.

She swiped her tears away and hollered to get its attention. "If you're looking for a makeover, give From Crud to Stud a try. We'll turn you around in no time."

She'd personally see to the creature's transformation. Work was all she had left. Weeping, she stumbled into the closet elevator and spoke to no one in particular. "Take me back, please."

The enclosure whooshed skyward so fast she had to hang on to the scorching grates to keep on her feet. Once the thing had shimmied to a gentle stop, Zoe couldn't let go. Head down, she scrunched her face, trying to stop her tears.

The door flew open on its own. Voices floated down the hall. She prayed it wasn't time to go back to work already. She needed a few moments, hours, days or weeks to pull herself together.

A zombie grunted. A reaper wailed.

Luck had abandoned her again. Freaking story of her life.

Defeated, she dragged out of the elevator, shoulders hunched. Three steps from her office, footfalls sounded from behind and stopped.

She willed whoever it was to go away.

"Zoe?" Becca.

Zoe ran her finger beneath her nose, slapped on a smile and turned, prepared to put on a show.

Becca's mouth sagged open. "Oh, my God, what happened?"

"Nothing. I mean, everything." She forced a laugh. "Had a great time."

"You're crying."

She sobbed uncontrollably and didn't fight Becca's embrace. Zoe clung to her as she had Anatol, Stefin and Taro on the platform when they'd still been interested in her.

"Sweetie." Becca stroked her hair. "Tell me what happened, please."

"Nothing. The guys were great. Best time I've ever had."

"And you're crying because of it?"

"These are happy tears, like Heather's."

Becca hugged her harder. "Where are the guys? Why didn't they come back with you? What happened, baby?"

"Nothing bad, really." They hadn't promised her the moon. She'd been a fool for falling so hard. "They just met some babes down there. Last I saw they were with them, having a good time. Hey, it's the second circle. That's why demons go there. To hook up and cut loose."

"They left you for other women?" Becca eased back and searched Zoe's face. "They refused to bring you back here?"

"Oh, hey, no. It wasn't like that at all." She smiled, striving for indifference, except for the tears streaming down her face. "They were busy. I didn't want to disturb them."

Becca clenched her jaw. "Why those—I warned them not to hurt you. They were supposed to see to your protection. At the very least stay by your side, like a decent demon would. Wait until I get my hands on—"

"No, no, no! Don't say anything to them. Don't interfere. You can't make them freaking love me." Zoe winced at the pain in her voice. "No one can. It's not their fault. I'm not who they want for the long run."

Becca looked helpless, the way she did whenever a potion stumped her or she didn't know what to say.

Just as well. Empty words weren't going to help Zoe now. "I need to get dressed. I want to be alone." She pulled away. "Please give me some time."

She ran into her office, closed and locked the door.

* * * *

If it wouldn't have taken too much time, Stefin would have vaporized Anatol and Taro. "This is on both of you."

"Us?" Taro clenched his jaw. "I didn't see you stop Zoe from leaving."

Anatol curled his upper lip. "Me, neither."

He shouldn't have had to. Stefin figured after giving Zoe some rest and stuffing her with more chocolate, she'd be good to go, not be fucking gone. They had searched everywhere for her, even going too close to the gated areas. If caught, there would have been hell to pay, literally.

Zoe wasn't anywhere. Desperate, Stefin strong-armed numerous demons, asking if they'd seen someone kidnap her. They hadn't. Outside the club, he cornered a strange creature that darted through the shadows on two legs and one arm.

"Does she work at From Crud to Stud?" The thing looked up at Stefin. "By the way, she offered me a makeover for free."

Ignoring that bold lie, Stefin bolted to the closet elevator.

Taro and Anatol were close behind.

Halfway to the office, Stefin remembered his nudity. The other guys finally noticed theirs. With no time to waste, they used their powers to dress in black shirts, pants and dress boots. Zoe wouldn't like them doing it the supernatural way, but Becca would surely freak if they paraded around in all their glory.

The enclosure bounced to a gentle stop. Stefin turned to the others. "I'll handle this."

"Oh, good." Anatol rolled his eyes. "That should make it turn out nicely."

Stefin got in his face. Anatol puffed out his chest. Taro made fists. The door swung open. Stefin bolted into the hall and stilled. Taro and Anatol bumped into him. He shouldered them away and considered running but couldn't.

Becca, Constance, MJ and Heather blocked him. The girls' arms were crossed over their chests, their mouths pressed into thin lines, way past pissed. Even sweet Heather tried like mad to frown.

"Ladies." Stefin poured on the charm. "If you'll excuse me."

"Not in this life." Becca uncrossed her arms and poked his chest. "I warned you what would happen if you even thought about hurting Zoe. Trust me. You're not pulling that crap around here." She glared at Anatol and Taro. "Neither are you two. You are so toast."

Stefin didn't understand, and then he did. "Zoe didn't come back here?" He couldn't imagine where in the fuck she could be.

"Of course, she came back." Constance glared. "We're her family. She needed comfort so she came to us."

"How could you?" Heather's mouth trembled.

MJ pulled Heather close and soothed her.

Stefin was totally lost. "I'm not following."

Constance looked at Becca. "Talk about hot but clueless."

He frowned. "Zoe's all right?"

"No." They'd spoken as one.

Becca was back to poking his chest. "You hurt her. You ripped her heart out and crushed her soul."

"How?" Zoe didn't have one. She was a freaking demon. Unless... He whirled on Anatol and Taro. "What did you do to Zoe?"

"Us?" Taro gave Stefin a dirty look. "Nothing. We were having a good time and then she disappeared."

"Ah, boys?" Constance pointed her bejeweled finger at them. "That's the problem. You were having a good time with other women. If you want to keep your balls, a little advice, leave with the one you brought."

Stefin wanted to screech. "We would have, but she left without us."

"We were letting her rest." Taro looked at the others. "Right?"

Anatol nodded. "All we did was talk to those female demons. We weren't doing anything."

"Even though they wanted that." Stefin shrugged. "Who could blame them, but I said no at least a hundred times."

Taro rapped his chest. "Two hundred for me."

Anatol laughed. "Such a pitiful amount for both of you. I passed a thousand easily."

Becca rubbed her temple. Constance shook her head. Heather's mouth trembled. MJ consoled.

Stefin wasn't going to waste another moment subjected to the ladies' cross-examination. "Where's Zoe?"

Constance pointed to the break room.

"Wait." Becca frowned. "I don't think you should bother her."

"That's okay, because we're not going to be doing that." Even if this got him banished to Hell, Stefin wasn't backing down. "We're going to talk. Meaning, this is between her and us, not you." He smiled sweetly. "Even though you mean well." He gestured to Taro and Anatol. "Let's go."

Zoe was at the table, her head down. She munched a Milky Way listlessly. Chocolate smears decorated her mouth.

Stefin wanted to lick her lips, but he didn't make any sudden moves. She'd put her schoolgirl outfit back on and had pulled her hair into such a tight ponytail her eyes were mere slits.

"*Chérie*." Anatol hurried into the room. He dropped to one knee at Zoe's feet. "I was so worried about you."

"Me, too." Taro hunkered down on her other side.

Stefin pulled the table away and crouched in front, his hands on her legs.

Zoe's chin wobbled.

Her sadness tore Stefin apart, more than all the other shit he'd been through. "Don't cry, please. There's no reason to. We didn't do anything."

She covered her eyes.

Anatol eased her hand away.

She smacked him.

Taro gestured in surrender.

Stefin wasn't about to. He wanted to settle this. "We were merely talking to those women."

Tears rolled down her cheeks. "While one was giving you a massage?" She turned to Anatol. "And two were playing with your dreadlocks?" She frowned at Taro. "And another stroked your arm?"

"Is that what you're upset about?" Stefin chuckled. "They wanted to do far more, but I refused at least five thousand times."

Taro hit his chest. "Ten thousand for me."

Anatol sniffed. "I lost count for myself at twenty thousand."

Zoe made a face. "Are you guys for real?"

She wanted the truth, not empty boasts. She wanted to feel special to them. Stefin got it. He came clean. "I was propositioned fifteen times. Sixteen if you count the male demon."

Taro slumped. "Thirteen for me."

"What does it matter?" Anatol twisted his dreadlocks. "We're here. We didn't do anything down there with anyone else."

Zoe didn't comment.

Stefin smacked Anatol's arm. "Tell her the truth. That's what she wants. You call her *chérie* and pretend you have finesse, but you're not willing to tell her the—"

"Understood, all right?" Anatol spoke to Zoe. "Six women propositioned me. There would have been more, but Stefin and Taro wouldn't let the others get close enough to do so."

Stefin shook his head.

Zoe barely controlled her tears. "You guys weren't tempted in the least?"

Taro looked surprised. "Not as we are with you."

Anatol smiled. "You're our Zoe."

Stefin nodded. "You belong to us. We're your Masters. How could it be any other way?"

Her shoulders shook from her hitching sobs. She struggled to speak. "I have to tell you something."

Stefin traded a glance with Taro and Anatol. They looked as worried as he felt. Surely, she wasn't going to banish them from her life because they'd been flirting a little. Very little for demons. Worried, he could barely speak. "What?"

"I love you guys. Don't tell me to take it back. I can't. I don't want to."

Stefin hugged Zoe before the others could, though they soon joined in. As one, they swayed from side to side.

"We love you, too." Stefin cleared the catch in his throat. He'd never known another woman like her. Feisty, exasperating, bullheaded, temperamental, loving, kind and thoughtful. Everything he'd always needed but had never had. "When we feared we'd lost you down there..." He couldn't finish.

Anatol kissed her palm. "Don't ever do that to us again."

Taro held her hand between his. "Or we'll beat your butt."

She giggled. "Take me, love me, please."

Now, she was talking the way Stefin liked.

The door to the break room slammed closed on its own. Before the sound had faded, he and the others had Zoe naked and stretched out on the table.

Epilogue

Nine months later…

The awards ceremony for staff, clients and supernatural vendors was approaching critical mass, only the most prestigious honors still not presented.

Zoe didn't expect any personal awards this year. For the first time since she'd joined From Crud to Stud, it didn't matter that no one would recognize her contributions to the business. She had exactly what she needed. Stefin, Taro and Anatol shared her table, looking handsome as sin in their tuxes, their powerful forms tamed for the evening though flames flickered mischievously in their eyes.

She gave her guys a sultry smile, reminding them what would come once they left this place. Domination. Bondage. Punishment. Pleasure.

For the moment, though, it wasn't a burden to be here. They'd each won an award for being the best new enforcer, their trophies well-deserved and beautifully designed by Heather. She'd outdone herself organizing the bash.

The banquet room was wonderfully opulent, boasting crystal chandeliers and French provincial furniture in dazzling gold and crimson. Carrion plants, Zoe's fave, graced her table rather than the floral centerpieces the others had. She stroked the fuzzy purple leaves, amused at how the waiter made a wide circle around the table. The way he held his breath told her he didn't care for the plant's unique fragrance or the sulfur scent inherent in demons.

His loss.

Seated at the next table were Daemon, Heather, MJ and four guys she'd invited to the bash—a were, vamp, reaper and warlock. While she flirted with them, Daemon and Heather gave each other sappy smiles, their love obvious. At the front table, Becca sat next to Eric and laughed softly at whatever he'd said. The high color in her cheeks told Zoe the comment must have been wicked. Good for them.

But bad for Constance. Poor thing shared Becca and Eric's table, the place setting for her date unused. The bum had stood her up. Anatol, Stefin and Taro had offered to hunt down the SOB and annihilate him, but Zoe had put the kibosh on that. No one, no matter how powerful, could force love on anyone. She understood that now and couldn't imagine hoping for anything different, as she once had with Ebenezer.

Adoration freely given was far nicer.

Stefin's calf brushed hers, so did Taro's. Anatol tapped his foot against her shoe. Each wanted to maintain a physical connection. Their devotion moved her in ways she hadn't dreamed and made her ache for Constance.

That did it. She had to brainstorm with Becca, Heather and MJ to find someone for Constance. It wasn't right that she was alone and so horny. She grinned at the twenty-something waiter. He smiled stiffly in return and fled. Didn't stop her from eyeing his tight ass.

"Excuse me, excuse me." The MC was on stage. He tapped his palm against the microphone.

High-pitched feedback tore through the room.

Groans broke out.

"Sorry." He stopped hitting the thing and even retracted his fangs.

He was one of their best success stories, the vamp who'd bitten Zoe the day she'd met her guys. What seemed a long time ago, yet also felt as if it had happened only yesterday.

The vamp read his cards and still looked lost, proving what an amateur he was at this. Not that it mattered. The nicest thing about these ceremonies was Becca including customers to cheer on their progress, and using their comments as the basis for staff awards. If the personnel didn't please them, there'd be no accolades.

Given how love had mellowed Zoe, she'd lost her mojo when it came to enforcing. Becca and the others didn't seem to mind. They accepted her for who she'd become. A demon mastered by tenderness, affection and scorching-hot sex.

"Okay, here we are." He held up a card. "Now pay attention. This honor goes to..."

Unable to wait a second longer, Zoe dug into her molten chocolate cake, savoring bite after decadent bite. It was an effort not to squeal.

Stefin, Anatol and Taro looked at her, their eyebrows lifted.

She must have made a noise without realizing it. Smiling sheepishly, she was about to enjoy another forkful when she noticed everyone in the room stared at her. Even the vamp waved his card, trying to get her attention.

"Sorry for making so much noise." She licked her lips. "I like chocolate."

Laughter rippled through the crowd.

Constance stood. "Get your butt up here for your award."

Zoe didn't understand.

"You've been voted best enforcer of all time." Becca gestured Zoe to the stage. "You're also the new manager of our enforcement team. That promotion comes with a hefty raise."

Her mouth sagged open.

Anatol bumped her shoulder. "A force to be reckoned with."

Taro grinned. "Beauty, brains and muscle."

"Our Zoe." Stefin winked.

Weeping, she pushed to her feet and hugged them fiercely.

The attendees applauded. *Girl on Fire* blasted from the sound system.

Blinking back tears, she strode to the stage. Her beaded red gown, an MJ creation, whispered around Zoe's curves.

She had those, too. Once she'd fallen in love and experienced its beauty, her appetite had picked up and she'd filled out. Her boobs and ass would never compete with JLo's, but she had enough to satisfy herself and her guys.

Filled with confidence and poise, she smiled at clients she'd wrestled to treatment tables and those she'd threatened when they hadn't behaved.

Each gave her a high five, thumbs-up or a broad grin, telling her she mattered, she wasn't a lonely demon any longer.

It felt good.

However, being cherished and loved by three sweet devils who were virile to the extreme, decadent as hell and precisely who she'd always needed was the absolute best.

Want to see more from this author?
Here's a taster for you to enjoy!

Taming the Beast:
Muzzing the Beast
Tina Donahue

Excerpt

"No, no, no—wait." The were folded his arms over his head, his face anguished.

Constance held back a frustrated sigh and dropped her hands. This was the sixth time she'd backed off this evening. The poor slob couldn't decide what memories he wanted her to remove and which he had to keep. "What's wrong now?"

"Everything." He curled into a fetal position on the treatment table, just about taking up residence in her office at From Crud to Stud, a New Orleans' makeover service for supernatural beings. "Give me a sec."

He'd already eaten up forty-five minutes of her shift with his indecision concerning a mortal babe who'd dumped him. Once she'd found out he was a were, she'd been history, no matter how much he'd tried to stifle his beastly urges. Given his animal lust for her, he'd ached to reminisce about every moment they'd been together, until he'd decided he hated her for the ultimate insult—she'd unfriended him on Facebook. Everyone had a breaking point. That was his and he needed her images excised from his brain until he didn't. Back and forth he'd gone, worse than a tween deciding what to wear to middle school.

Constance was a voodoo priestess, not his mom. "Sweetie, I have other clients. You need to make up your mind."

He tightened his arms. "I. Am. Trying."

"Not hard enough." She wanted to smack him upside his head.

She'd already had a worse day than his. Make that a month. Hell, years. Why kid herself? She'd been dating since she was fourteen but wasn't any closer to a grand romance now than she'd been back then. For thirteen years, she'd slogged through countless hookups and fixups that landed her with guys who were the proverbial frogs rather than princes, none interested in her for the long haul. Three weeks ago had been her Waterloo. Radagar, the warlock she'd been dating on a regular basis, had showed up for their night out with another babe hanging on his arm.

The young woman had grinned and wiggled her fingers at Constance, like they were buddies or something.

Given that he and the girl had been almost welded together, Constance hadn't been in the mood to wiggle back. As the only sane one in the group, she'd had to ask the obvious. *'Did you forget this is your and my date night or did you confuse my apartment for being the restaurant where we're supposed to be going?'*

He'd laughed. *'You're too funny. This is Katka. She just turned nineteen.'*

And had looked way younger, which had made Constance feel like Methuselah. Why Radagar had seemed happy about that had eluded her. Of course, he'd never been much in the brains department. Being a hunk and competent in bed was all she'd asked from him—with a little fidelity on the side, such as not being with other women when they were together. *'Why is she here?'*

'I thought we'd liven things up.' He'd swatted Katka's butt playfully. *'She's the newest member of our team.'*

As if they'd been coworkers rather than lovers. Since Constance hadn't been up for a threesome or more when even newer members had joined the team, she'd broken up with him on the spot, slammed the door in his shocked face and eaten a tub of Häagen-Daz Belgian Chocolate ice cream for dinner chased by Dove miniatures for dessert. That turned out to be the best date night she'd ever had.

Maybe I should give up on men and switch to… Naw, that wasn't going to happen. She was attracted to the opposite sex, while they couldn't seem to disappoint her enough.

Her intercom buzzed then crackled.

"Ah, can you come up here? Now? Right now? This very second in fact?" Heather, the receptionist and Constance's BFF, sounded more unglued than usual. "Sorry I have to ask, really I am, but please, can you come up here? Please?"

As a good fairy and an empathetic healer, Heather was always super polite and apologetic as hell, yet this seemed beyond serious…like maybe a mortal had stumbled into this place. On the few occasions that had happened, Heather had had strict instructions—call Constance to take care of the problem. If the dude or dudine left with memories that involved weres howling and vamps hissing, everyone who worked here was toast.

She spoke into the intercom. "Be right there."

"Thank you." Heather panted. "I mean, really, I am so grateful you're—"

"You bet." She hurried to her office door.

"Hey." The were pushed to a sitting position on the padded table. "What about me?"

She'd forgotten his turmoil. "Hold still."

"What — no — wait."

Constance couldn't. She gripped his head and did the only thing she could. She removed his memories of her.

He blinked then frowned. "Who are you?"

"The site medic. You fainted during treatment."

He gripped her wrist and regarded her shadowed, sensuous office. Wispy smoke rose from incense sticks on her desk. Candlelight glinted off beaded curtains and created colorful dots on the ceiling and walls. "How'd I get in here?"

"Couple of the enforcers carried you in from the other room. Don't you dare leave until I get back to make sure you're okay."

He spied her laptop. "While you're gone, do you mind if I use your computer to get on Facebook? There's something I have to check out."

Of course, he did. Poor thing hoped his ladylove had friended him again, and if she hadn't, he could leave a nasty message using Constance's ISP address. "Be my guest."

The intercom buzzed. "Are you coming? Please?"

"Yeah, right away." Constance pointed her bejeweled finger at him. "Hang tight."

She raced down the hall and stopped short before reaching the reception area. Its coral walls, gas light fixtures, faux brick floor, numerous potted plants and feathery ferns created an earthy and romantic feel, which screamed mortal to fool the unsuspecting who happened inside.

This one must be pure awful. Heather stood behind her chair, possibly for protection, digging her nails into the leather, her face ashier than usual. Its tint matched her pale blonde hair and signature white clothing.

Constance edged around the corner, leery and curious as to whoever had scared the bejeezus out of Heather.

The guy faced Constance, but his gaze was on the ceiling. Thankfully, no vamp had morphed into a bat and was buzzing around up there.

Despite the steamy summer night, he wore a blue suit, white shirt and gray tie, the clothes draping him beautifully. Deliciously tall, he had to be six three or better, broad in the shoulders, his hips narrow, his build lean yet muscular.

Warmth filled her when it shouldn't have. Radagar's stupid stunt had cured her of men for a long, long time. Then again… She clutched her full-length gown since it wouldn't be polite to grab this guy. What a hottie. He wore his curly black hair cropped short. His cinnamon-colored skin was a stunning contrast to his light blue eyes, his features masculine and a trifle rough.

Her pulse quickened.

She guessed him to be Creole, early thirties, an executive and probably mortal given Heather's reaction. Most women would have been drooling by now, not hyperventilating. In another few seconds, she might be out cold and Constance would have to give her CPR. She would have preferred to do that for him.

To break the ice, she inched closer. "Well, hey, there."

He took her in from stem to stern, his attention snagging on her saffron-colored turban and matching gown then lingering on her mouth and boobs. Like he couldn't help himself.

She wasn't about to complain. Call her crazy, but the lovely bulge behind his fly seemed to thicken in interest.

Her pussy creamed in response.

Heather wasn't as taken. With him turned away from her, she waved her arms in what looked like warning.

Constance couldn't imagine why. For her to cup his good-looking head and remove his memories of this place would be more play than work.

He met her gaze. "Evening."

His rumbling baritone registered clear to her tongue and tonsils. She smiled.

Male interest sparkled in his gorgeous eyes. He killed his arousal and got ultra-serious. "I'm Detective Gabe Legrand."

Constance's heart stuttered. He couldn't mean as in a freaking cop but probably did. Her smile went kaput over what had brought him here. Not to mention what would happen if others in his department suspected something weird was going on within these walls. "You're with the police?"

He lifted a small leather wallet that displayed a silver shield, its crescent engraved with a word, maybe *detective*. The thing was too far away for her to read. Beneath the crescent was a star with another word and a number.

She wouldn't have been surprised if it was 007, considering his awesome looks.

He pocketed his badge and advanced with stunning grace, similar to an animal in the wild stalking its prey. God help her, she was still more tempted than alarmed and drifted toward him in what seemed like slow motion. Another step and they'd touch. She didn't see the harm.

He stopped. "You're the owner?"

Heather made a pained sound. "Constance is a good person."

Not that good. His woodsy-musky scent warmed her as the sun never had and made her legs watery.

"Your name is Constance?"

"Guilty as charged." She hoped a joke would lighten the moment so Heather wouldn't faint or blurt the truth about this place since good fairies couldn't lie. "Nice to meet you, Detective. Or can I call you Gabe?" She offered her hand.

His own was so large it swallowed hers, his palm dry and slightly callused, his grip firm but not intimidating.

Heaven in a handshake. She liked a man who took charge, in particular when it came to bedroom play. Not that a roll between the sheets seemed possible, given his slight frown.

"I thought Becca Salt owned this place." He spoke to Heather. "Didn't I ask you to call the owner up here?"

Heather gripped her chair so hard her knuckles got even whiter. "Uh-huh."

"Then why didn't you?"

She clenched her jaw.

Before she broke her molars, Constance jumped in. "She did. I'm the owner. Constance Salt."

Gabe regarded with suspicion, though his attention did wander to her mouth, boobs and her hand as she released his. "Then who's Becca Salt? The name listed on the permits and other papers as the owner."

"Still me." Constance leaned toward him as if to share a big, bad secret. "My first name's Becca, but I hate it, so I go by my middle name with coworkers and friends." She gave him a sweet smile and gestured to the hall. "Why don't we go to my office to talk?"

Rather than follow her, he glanced past.

Becca strolled toward them. Her silky blue halter-top and harem pants shimmered beneath the lights, as did her jewelry. Silver stars dangled from her navel, dainty chains decorated one ankle and rings glittered on her toes. Coupled with her flame-red hair, alabaster skin and the heavy Goth makeup she wore around her eyes, she was one of a kind. Not to mention a witch, in the literal not figurative sense.

"Lorraine." Constance glared at Becca. "What are you doing roaming around? Have you finished the accounts? You need to do those payables tonight."

Becca halted, took in the scene and lingered on Gabe. She got paler than Heather, most likely because she figured something was way wrong. "Uh, sorry. Won't happen again." She pivoted and hurried away.

"Whoa. Wait. You're going in the wrong direction." Constance pointed to her own office. "Do your work in your spot, not mine."

With the were still inside her space, Constance couldn't bring Gabe in there.

"Right." Becca offered a sheepish smile and raced toward Constance's office.

Gabe's face masked whatever he thought. "She's your accountant?"

"A nice person generally, but... Let's face it, good help is so hard to find these days. Follow me."

A were, maybe hers, let out an ear-piercing howl. The vamps chorused their hisses. Demons' growls and grunts joined in.

Eyes wide, Gabe shoved his hand inside his jacket.

Constance would have bet he was reaching for his gun, not his badge.

He turned from side to side, neck craned, gaze searching. "What in the hell's going on here?"

"Therapy."

"What?"

She affected her most professional demeanor. "That's all I can say. It's all I will say even if you have a warrant.

There is such a thing as shrink-client confidentiality, you know."

The were bellowed.

Gabe kept his hand inside his jacket. "Shrink? That's what you call your so-called therapists?"

Talk about hurtful. "I'm as laid-back as they come." Constance ran a tapered nail over her jawline. She liked his stubble and wanted to stroke it. "No need to use big words, now is there?"

"Exactly what kind of therapy do you do here?"

"The usual."

"Meaning?"

"Let's discuss it in my office." She gestured to Becca's.

He stayed where he was. "Why not here?"

She wanted to be alone with him. Odd. Mortals had never appealed to her, which made him uber special. "Because." It was the only answer she could come up with. He'd fried her brain with his scent, occupation and great looks.

He eyed her skeptically. "Because of what?"

Time to get tough, or as much as she could with an Adonis like him. "Ah… confidentiality. Only staff and clients are allowed in the reception area. Since you're neither, and our clients aren't expecting a stranger, you'll have to follow me."

Sign up for our newsletter and find out about all our romance book releases, eBook sales and promotions, sneak peeks and FREE romance books!

About the Author

Tina is an Amazon and international bestselling novelist who writes passionate romance for every taste–'heat with heart'–for traditional publishers and indie. Booklist, Publisher's Weekly, Romantic Times and numerous online sites have praised her work. She's won Readers' Choice Awards, was named a finalist in the EPIC competition, received a Book of the Year award, The Golden Nib Award, awards of merit in the RWA Holt Medallion competitions, and second place in the NEC RWA contests. She's featured in the Novel & Short Story Writer's Market. Before penning romances, she worked at a major Hollywood production company in Story Direction.

Tina loves to hear from readers. You can find her contact information, website details and author profile page at https://www.totallybound.com

www.ingramcontent.com/pod-product-compliance
Lightning Source LLC
Chambersburg PA
CBHW020410180626
46812CB00003B/915